CANYON OF DEATH

A Yakima Henry Western

PETER BRANDVOLD

WOLFPACK PUBLISHING
— EST 2013 —

Published in the United States by Wolfpack Publishing,
Las Vegas

Wolfpack Publishing
5130 S. Fort Apache Road, 215-380
Las Vegas, NV 89148

wolfpackpublishing.com

Paperback ISBN 978-1-64734-626-3
eBook ISBN 978-1-64734-625-6

CANYON OF DEATH

1

Julia Taggart rolled toward Yakima Henry on the large, canopied bed in Yakima's private room at the Conquistador Inn in Apache Springs, Arizona Territory.

The single white sheet slipped down far enough that he could see she wasn't wearing a stitch. Her rich chestnut hair was pinned atop her head, sausage curls dangling down against her cheeks. Her full, pale, pink-tipped breasts sloped toward the mattress as she scuttled toward him. The Town Marshal of Apache Springs sucked a slow breath, filling up his lungs, tensing his entire body.

How he'd yearned with a near-savage desperation to hold this beautiful, beguiling woman again in his arms and to never let her go...

He turned his head away from her as she pressed her cheek against the small of his back and snaked her left arm around his waist. She splayed the fingers of that hand across his flat belly, over his red-and-black calico shirt still dusty and sweaty from the long trail to and from the stagecoach that the Apaches had run down.

His old deputy, the Rio Grande Kid was safe for now, over at Doc Sutton's place. The stage passengers were safe, as well. At least, those who'd survived the Chiricahuas' attack. Yakima's junior deputy, Galveston Penny, was asleep in Yakima's office, only a few drunks in the cells flanking the young ex-cow puncher. All was well in Apache Springs to which the railroad had just come. All was well…for now. Yakima had time for a little personal enjoyment.

Julia groaned and lowered her splayed hand to just above the large brass buckle of his cartridge belt, digging her fingers in, kindling a fire in the big half-breed's loins.

"Get undressed, Yakima," she said, pressing her soft lips against his back. "I don't care what my sister means to you. I'll be *goddamned* if I just don't care!" Julia, whose father owned the Conquistador Hotel & Saloon, managed the place herself. It would have been easy for her to slip into his room even if he hadn't locked it.

Yakima looked down at the hand on his belly.

He wanted desperately to grab that hand and turn to her and give her what she so urgently wanted but he'd be damned if he could do it. She'd been teasing him by sending her whores to his room, a different one every night. Tantalizing him, mocking his goatish male desires, and trying to keep him away from her younger sister, Emma. Thus, he couldn't have been more surprised to find the willow, chestnut-haired, gray-eyed creature here now herself…in his bed.

He squeezed her hand and thrust it back behind him.

"Get out, Julia." Yakima rose from the bed and in two strides he was in the chair by the door. He doffed his hat, let it tumble onto the floor, and, leaning forward, his head nearly to his knees, he ran a big, copper paw through his long, coal-black hair. "Get out!"

She stared at him in shock, her gray eyes wide, touched by the pearl dawn light angling through a window behind her. Her lower jaw hung. It was as though he'd slapped her across her beautiful face. She didn't say anything. She just knelt there, naked save for one arm drawn across her breasts. A tender nipple peeked out from between her fingers.

Yakima looked up at her from beneath his black eyebrows mantling almond-shaped, jade eyes set deep in a darkly-chiseled, severely-featured face with the high, tapering cheekbones of his Cheyenne mother. The green eyes, clear as a high-mountain lake, were compliments of his prospector father's Old-World German lineage. They were sometimes cast as softly as a spring rain in a meadow, sometimes forged as hard as diamonds, glinting with the savagery of his Cheyenne warrior ancestors. He stared back at the raving, naked beauty on the bed before him, trying to bring that savage sharpness to his gaze but unable to get them out of that rainy spring meadow.

Julia saw the lie in those eyes.

Slowly, she shook her head. "You don't want that."

She dropped her arms from his breasts. She unfolded one long, alabaster leg in turn, placing her long, delicate feet onto the Oriental carpeted floor and walked over to him, knocking his sweaty black hat aside as she knelt between his wide-spread knees.

She placed a hand on each knee. She shook her head again.

"No," she said knowingly, able to read him like a book. "That's not what you want."

"Yes, it is," he said without conviction, again lowering his hand and running a hand through his sweat-damp hair. Putting some steel in his voice as well as flint in his eyes, he said, "Get out of here."

"Why?"

"I don't want you here."

Julia glanced down between his spread knees and said with a caustic laugh, "You and I both know that isn't true."

He closed his legs and wrapped his hands around her wrists, lifting them off his knees and pushing her back away from him, keeping her wrists in his hands. Her breasts jostled against her chest, rose and fell sharply as she breathed. He took his eyes off of them.

"Get out of here. I won't tell you again."

"What is it? What's happened?"

Raising his voice and hardening his jaws, Yakima said, "Get out of here, Julia!"

"What has happened?"

"It's your…" He struggled to get the words out. Each one pierced his heart like a bayonet. "It's your sister."

She stared at him. He couldn't meet her gaze.

Again, she shook her head, narrowed one eye shrewdly. "I told you…I don't care. You can have her, too. I don't care."

"Yes, you do."

"No, I don't. I know you don't love her. Maybe you love to meet her out in the desert on your trysts after sunset. You like to lay with her. You enjoy punishing her with…" She let her eyes flick at his midsection. "But you don't love her. You love me, Yakima. We both know it. I saw it in your eyes earlier. It's true if anything in this world has ever been true before!"

She leaped up off her knees and pressed her mouth against his. He tried to push her away, but he couldn't do it. She pressed her mouth harder against him, opened his lips with her own. Groaning, she slid her tongue between his lips.

Yakima felt his body yielding. His hands opened. She grabbed one of his with both of hers, placed it against her right breast as she kissed him with an urgent hunger, the nipple turning hard against his calloused palm.

He opened his mouth and began returning her passionate kiss, lapping at her tongue, her teeth...but then he remembered that damned wanted circular her father was blackmailing him with, and he summoned the strength out of the dark depths of his soul. He pulled his head back from hers, lifted his hand from her swollen breast, placed both of his hands on her upper arms.

He shoved her away from him, hardening his jaws and gritting his teeth. "It's over, Julia. We can't see each other anymore. I'm sorry for harassing you, trying to get you entangled in me again. It was wrong. We can't be together and that's final."

"No!"

She lurched up toward him again. This time he shoved her away with more power than he'd intended. She flew backward, dropping onto her bottom and falling back against the bed.

She gazed up at him hurtfully, her flushed cheeks turning ashen. She drew a deep breath and said slowly, "What has happened? What has gotten into you?"

Yakima had been only vaguely aware of running footsteps in the hall outside his door. Now they were growing louder. So loud that he had to raise his voice to say to Julia, "Ask your father. He'll tell you the whole thing. That'll take care of it. You'll realize then that it has to be over between us. You have to move on, Julia."

She stared at him in exasperation and shock as the footsteps fell silent. They were replaced by a loud hammering on his door. "Yakima! Marshal Henry!" It was the voice of his junior deputy, Galveston Penny. "Come quick, Marshal. Julian Barnes was stabbed somethin' awful over at Senora Galvez's place, an' the ranny who cut him's on the run!"

2

Yakima would have welcomed a distraction from the
emotional mud bath that he and Julia had just taken together. But not the kind of a distraction his young deputy
had just shouted through his door. Not the murder of one
of Apache Springs' most prominent businessmen.

"Hold on," he said to the door.

Yakima rose from the chair. He ripped a sheet off the
bed and wrapped it around Julia slumped on the floor
before him, looking up at him incredulously, hurtfully,
her hair now hanging in a tattered bun down over one
pale shoulder.

He lifted her to her feet and led her to one side of the
door. He opened the door, concealing Julia with it, and
gazed at Galveston Penny, the skinny, tow-headed young
deputy in a store-bought, ill-fitting suit standing before
him, eyes bright with alarm.

The kid, in his early twenties, flung an arm out, gesturing down the hall toward the stairs. "Marshal Henry, Julian Barnes was stabbed over at—"

"I heard!" Yakima crouched to retrieve his hat from the floor and then picked up his Winchester Yellowboy repeater from where he'd leaned it against the wall.

Young Penny stared through the door saying haltingly, "He took off like a bat out of hell. You, uh...you, uh...want me to get after him?" The deputy sounded about as eager to go after the killer as he was to saddle a grizzly. "It's uh...it's Gabriel Mankiller." He swallowed.

Yakima rested his rifle on his shoulder and reached for the doorknob. As he did, he glanced at the deputy still standing in the open doorway.

Penny was staring at a pair of ladies' lacey pink pantalettes lying on the floor near the bed, which was where Julia must have dropped them when she'd arrived and undressed.

Galveston turned to Yakima and with a faint, wry curl of his mouth and with humor flashing in his eyes, said, "I mean...if'n you're busy an' all..."

"Oh, shut up—I'm not busy!"

Galveston stumbled back into the hall, flushing. "Well, hell—I didn't mean nothin' by it. I just..."

Yakima grabbed the door and started to pull it closed as he stepped into the hall. He stopped and met Julia's gaze through the crack between the wall and the other end of the door, between the hinges. Her gaze held his for a split second as she pressed the sheet against her bosom.

Yakima cursed under his breath and continued into the hall, drawing the door closed behind him.

He hurried down the hall toward the stairs, Galveston trotting along beside him, trying to match his stride. "I just meant," the kid said, "you know...I mean...I figured them under-frillies weren't yours, Marshal Henry." He chuckled and glanced sidelong at his taller, darker boss.

Yakima sobered him quickly with a look.

"Uh...sorry," Galveston said.

"Gabriel Mankiller, you said?"

"That's right. He stabbed him upstairs at Senora Galvez's place. There was another fella with him—that Mex you hauled in last week for slappin' down that Chinaman tracklayer."

"Damaso Guzman," Yakima recalled. He also recalled that Guzman was the type of sidewinder he'd figured he'd have to turn the key on again.

"Yeah, that...that's the one! Got a big snarling wildcat tattooed on his forehead. Carries two knives on his belt, another in a sheath on his chest."

"Right wholesome fella, Guzman. You know why they attacked Barnes?"

"The doxie Barnes was with said Mankiller grabbed

Mister Barnes's wallet off a dresser and lit a shuck with Guzman. A witness to the attack, passing in the hallway at the time of the incident, corroborated Miss Ella's story."

Yakima arched a brow at his young deputy, impressed. "'Corroborated', eh?"

Galveston grinned. "Yes, sir. I heard the county attorney bandy that one around in court the other day."

They were tramping down the broad carpeted stairs, dropping into the Conquistador Inn's main, smartly outfitted drinking hall with a large horseshoe bar cleaving the room down its middle. No lamps had been lighted yet, so shadows reigned. The chairs were tipped over atop the tables. The place wouldn't open until seven o'clock though one of Julia's barmen was milling around behind the mahogany, stocking shelves warily and yawning.

"What's the commotion?" the barman, whose name was Ivor Ingersoll, asked as Yakima and Galveston hurried toward the front door.

Galveston turned to yell anxiously, "Mister Barnes was stabbed in the back by that big Apache, Gabriel Man—"

He stopped when Yakima elbowed him. "Stay focused here, Galveston." He pulled open the front door and stepped outside, turning to his skinny junior deputy moving out behind him, and asking, "How bad off is Barnes?"

"All I know is he was screamin' awful bad when I was over at the Senora's place, and there was blood all over the bed. The poor girl he was diddlin' when Mankiller sunk that knife in his back was curled up on the floor, looking more red than white!"

"Was she injured, too?"

"No, just scared out of her wits, I think. Which is understandable, if you ask me. Can you imagin' lay there starin' up at the ceilin' waitin' for your jake to… you know…an' then seein' that big Injun come in and—"

"Galveston—stay focused, son!"

"Sorry, Marshal!"

"Did you send for the doc?"

"Of course!"

"Did Mankiller and Guzman ride out together?"

"That's what I was told—yessir!"

"How long ago and in which direction?"

"Ten minutes." Galveston flung his arm to indicate west. "That way!"

Yakima glanced at a zebra dun he thought was Galveston's tied to a hitchrack fronting the Conquistador. It was the only horse on the street at this early hour. "Is that your hay burner?"

"Of course. You wouldn't expect me to walk the two blocks over here from the jailhouse, would you?" There was no irony in the younker's tone.

"No, no—of course not. I'm gonna take your horse." Yakima walked over to the zebra and pulled the old

Winchester carbine from the saddle scabbard and tossed it to Galveston. "Take your rifle. Go back over to the Senora's place and gather as many witnesses together as you can, and note what they tell you. Write it down. The way things are goin' around here"—he cast a quick glance at the two shiny silver rails running down the dead center of the town's main drag, leaving about thirty open yards between the rails and the opposing business establishments on each side of the street—"we're gonna have to start following the book as close as we can. The lawbook, I mean. We're gonna need all the evidence we can get when we talk to the circuit judge about this deal."

As he swung up onto Galveston's horse, Yakima scoffed at how civilized the town was becoming. At least, it was becoming more populated. The more people, the more "progress" coming to Apache Springs in the wake of gold being discovered in and around the Sierra Estrada in the western foothills of which the booming town sat, Yakima had noted a definite decline in actual civility.

The current incident with Barnes was just more evidence.

"You should gather a posse, maybe, Yakima," Galveston said as he gazed leerily up at the tall half-breed straddling his horse. "I mean, that Mankiller's name is right fittin', I heard tell. And Guzman." The young man shook his head. "He's just as *bad.*"

"No time for a posse." Yakima reined the zebra west along the town's main street. "Keep the lid on the town—will ya, Galveston? I'll be back as soon as I can!"

"Be careful, Marshal!" the deputy called.

Yakima booted the zebra into a lope between the rails that shone with more and more definition to his left, as the sun inched up the horizon to the east, behind him.

He followed the trail on out of the ragged outskirts of the town, whose edges were stretching farther and farther out into the rolling desert spiked with greasewood and ocotillo and the finger-shaped sentinels of saguaro cactus. As the sun rose, shadows stretched across the rocky desert along both sides of the wagon trail, which was a floury line curving and foreshortening into the misty distance beyond Yakima.

The Dragoons were a long, dun-colored razor-back stretched out ahead of him, gaining more and more definition as the light grew. The Sierra Estrada, a spur range jutting off the western edge of the Chiricahuas, fell back behind him.

For three miles the trail followed the two silver rails of the Central Arizona Company's spur line, which connected Apache Springs with Benson and Tucson and all points west and east—to so-called "civilization" itself. Yakima had liked the town much better when he'd drifted here two years ago, just wanting to cool his heels after a bout of bad trouble up north, and break a few rocks in his own quest for a modest El Dorado.

He'd intended to continue on south to Mexico, but then one damn thing had led to another, he'd gotten entangled with not one but two women—sisters, no less— and here he was, forking a cayuse in pursuit of outlaws and wearing a five-pointed star on his shirt, beneath the lapel of his black frock coat.

Yakima Henry—lawdog. Imagine that.

He snorted a disbelieving laugh as he rode crouched low in the saddle, gazing down at the floury trail marked with the indentations of two distinct sets of shod horse tracks. Recent tracks. Both sets of prints were less than a half-hour old.

He was on the right trail. His quarry wasn't far.

As he rode, the sun rose behind him, the heat intensifying. It was so dry that his sweat evaporated at nearly the same time it oozed from his pores, leaving a salty crust on top of that he'd acquired when he'd ridden out to help his senor deputy, the Rio Grande Kid, and the Apache-stalked stage on which the Kid had been hauling a prisoner back from Tucson.

Fifteen minutes out of Apache Springs, the twin rails of the Central Arizona Line swerved off to the right, crossing an arroyo via a new wooden bridge that still stank of the coal oil bathing its timbers. As the trail swerved to the left, south, around a rocky hogback straight ahead, Yakima glanced down at the finely churned dirt.

The fresh tracks remained. So far, the riders hadn't felt the need to head cross-country to avoid a possible hunter or hunters. They had to know they'd be trailed. You didn't knife a man as important as Julian Barnes and not think there'd be serious repercussions. Even in a town growing as fast as Apache Springs and in which the local law enforcement was seriously undermanned.

Barnes was one of the newcomers to town, arriving a little over a year ago to build his almost instantly notorious Bella Union Theater on Third Avenue, where some of the most popular dancing girls on the frontier pranced around on stage wearing no more than hair feathers and smiles. (Barnes even put on Shakespeare plays fully cast by nude women. Who cared if it didn't make sense? The cowboys and miners wouldn't have known Shakespeare from General Grant's three-legged cat.)

Apparently, Barnes didn't like to mix business with pleasure, however, so instead of allowing his own doxies at the Bella Union to tend his male cravings, he headed over to Senora Alvarez's brothel on the main drag and satisfied himself in the Senora's nattily appointed love nests on the second and third floors of the gaudy Victorian structure. And that was where the man got stuck by the big half-breed Apache, Gabriel Mankiller.

Something didn't seem right about the whole affair.

Why attack and rob a man of Barnes's stature, especially when there were witnesses? Of course, there'd likely been whiskey involved, and whiskey trumped good sense every day of the week, especially in a boom town like Apache Springs. But, still…something about the mess nagged at the edges of Yakima's consciousness though he didn't dwell on it over long.

First things first—and that first thing was running down Mankiller and his companero, Damaso Guzman.

Yakima loped along the base of the rocky bluff, angling southwest, the high butte sliding back behind his right shoulder. Another high nest of rocks rose off the trail's left side—a long, red, vaguely dogleg-shaped dyke appropriately named the Dogleg Rocks. In the past, before the railroad had come to town, stagecoaches between Tombstone and/or Tucson and Apache Springs were frequently robbed near the Rocks, which provided good cover for highwaymen.

Something told Yakima that he himself should be wary of the Rocks now, too. He checked the blowing zebra dun down to a walk and, holding the reins firmly in his gloved hands, squinted against the intensifying, brassy desert light as he scrutinized the disheveled formation rising thirty or so yards off the trail, above the bristling desert flora.

A slight breeze erupted, moaning through the rocks and lifting dust from a clearing amongst the greasewood and yucca, shepherding the grit to the southeast. Yakima perused the Dogleg Rocks through that billowing tan curtain, apprehension touching his spine like the cold tip of a witch's finger.

Movement in the brush to his hard left quickened his heart. His heart slowed when he saw merely a coyote slinking through the chaparral. Yakima's ticker quickened yet again when the coyote tossed a wary glance back over its right shoulder, toward the Rocks.

Yakima stopped Galveston Penny's dun as he returned his gaze to the high, ragged dyke that was likely the result of pitching and breaking plates of earth several billion years ago.

"What is it?" he asked the coyote too quietly for anyone but himself to hear. Slowly, Yakima reached forward and slid his Yellowboy repeater from the saddle scabbard. "What you runnin' from, feller? What you see up in them rocks...?"

Just then sunlight glinted from a notch about halfway up the dyke.

Yakima hurled himself off the dun's back as the angry whine of a bullet shredded the air over the now-empty saddle and was followed a half-second later with the hiccupping belch of a rifle.

Yakima struck the trail hard and rolled into the brush as the zebra dun whinnied shrilly, then wheeled and galloped back in the direction they'd come from, reins bouncing along the ground behind it.

Another bullet...and then another...and another plunked into the ground near Yakima.

He continued rolling deeper into the chaparral, sucking a sharp breath through his teeth when he got too close to a cholla, or leaping cactus, and ended up with a handful of the short, nasty cream bristles bristling from his right bicep. He brushed off the spikes with his gloved left hand then rolled up behind a rock as a bullet slammed into the rock's face with a deafening *whang!*

Another bullet caromed over Yakima's right shoulder to plunk into a barrel cactus with a hollow thud.

Yakima had lost his hat in his tumble from the saddle.

Now he shook his long hair back from his face and edged a careful look around his covering rock's left side and across the chaparral to the doglegging dyke. Two smoke puffs shone as the two shooters continued cutting down on him, the next two bullets clipping a branch from a creosote shrub just ahead of him and spanging off a rock behind his left shoulder.

Yakima drew his head down behind the rock, gritting his teeth.

Mankiller and Guzman meant business.

He was glad to have gotten a look, even a brief one, at the dyke they were shooting from. He had a reasonably good sense of where both shooters were. One was hunkered in that notch Yakima had spied earlier, near the trail end of the dyke and about halfway between the bottom and the crest.

The other man was a little lower down and maybe twenty feet away from the first, farther out from the trail.

They were close. Damned close. Maybe seventy yards away.

The trouble was, they had the high ground and Yakima was hunkered down here on the desert floor with sparse cover. He didn't think they'd be able to keep up flinging lead at the rate they were flinging it, however. Not without running out of ammo. The bullets were slicing through the air all around him and hammering his covering rock resoundingly, angrily. In the frenzied shots, Yakima sensed the killers' frustration at not having blown him out of his saddle when they'd first drawn a bead on him.

Fortunately for him, the sun had flashed off what he'd presumed was a rifle barrel. And he'd been right. This wasn't his first rodeo. If it had been, and he'd dismissed that reflection, he'd likely be sporting a third eye for his witlessness.

As he'd suspected it would, the shooting tapered off.

Silence fell over the shallow natural bowl in the desert that the marshal of Apache Springs now found himself in, with two killers perched in the rocks above.

Yakima peered around the rock's right side, exposing his right eye. Ready to pull his head back if he saw another puff of smoke, he gazed up at the ridge.

No more smoke shone. No bullets came.

Had his ambushers decided to be a little more judicial in their bullet placements, or had they pulled out?

Only one way to find out.

Keeping his torso low to the ground, Yakima pulled his knees up beneath him, setting his heels in the ground. He drew a breath, squeezed the Yellowboy in his right hand, then gave a grunt as he leaped up off his heels and bolted out from behind the rock, running hard to the right then diving for another, large rock maybe fifteen yards beyond the first one.

A bullet chewed into the ground just inches off his flying heels.

As he hit the ground and rolled, the rifle crack reached his ears, echoing around the hollow. Another bullet ricocheted off the large covering rock with an ear-rattling, girl-like scream.

Yakima sat on his butt and pressed his back against the rock's hard, cool surface, holding the Yellowboy up and down in both hands.

Well, they hadn't pulled out. That much he knew.

Good. At least, he thought it was good. But they still had the high ground. That was a definite problem.

Now he could wait for the two bushwhackers to grow impatient and to come to him, where they'd be on even ground, or he could go to them. That was a tricky alternative, there being sparse cover between him and them. If he waited for them to come to him, however, they might pull out, and then he'd be back where he'd started—tracking them.

There was no telling how far Galveston's horse had run. All the way back to Apache Springs, for all Yakima knew.

Best to run his quarry to ground, though at the moment it looked more like Yakima was *their* quarry.

Oh, well. This wasn't his first rodeo. He'd turned the

tables on killers before. Take Bill Thornton, for instance, the son of a bitch who'd murdered Yakima's wife, Fay.

No.

This was no time to go down memory lane. Yakima had to stay right here, right now. Fay was dead. He'd buried her years ago, and he had to move on. If one thing coming to Apache Springs had helped him with, it was with moving on. Letting go of the past and realizing it was possible for him to fall in love again. Faith would understand. In fact, she'd have wanted him to do just that.

It was just too bad he'd fallen in love with the wrong damned woman with the wrong damned father wielding a very inconvenient wanted circular...

Yakima was moving now to the southwest, imitating a snake writhing its way across the desert floor. The thoughts sifting through his brain were vague whisperings in his ears. He closed the door on them now as he came to a patch of cleared ground that he'd soon have to negotiate his way across most delicately if he wanted to be spared a bad case of lead poisoning.

He stopped and peered to his left, toward the dyke. He had a limited view of the dogleg formation between a short, broad barrel cactus and a tall ocotillo poking its octopus tendrils skyward. From his position, so low to the ground and not wanting to raise his head and risk getting it shot off, he couldn't see the ambushers' positions.

That was all right.

He assumed they were trying to track him with their rifles. If so, they'd get a glimpse of him in a second.

He drew his knees up again, drew another deep breath, and vaulted up and forward. He ran across the small clearing, keeping his head down, scissoring his arms and legs, his long hair whipping wildly about his head. After six long strides he hurled himself off his heels again, launching into a dive.

He hit the ground behind a covering of brush and scattered rocks, rolling, wondering why more bullets had not come, probing the air for him, the rifles on the dyke screaming like witches on All Hallows Eve.

There was only the high whine of insects emphasizing the desert's surreal silence.

An eerie silence.

Yakima almost would have preferred gunfire. At least, he'd have a good estimation of his stalkers' positions. But now he didn't know where in the hell they were. Were they moving toward him or away from him? Maybe they were pulling out, heading on down to Mexico or north to Tucson and Phoenix, maybe intending to get lost even farther north, on the Mogollon Rim.

Or maybe they were moving in for the kill…

From somewhere ahead came a sound. A very furtive sound, and not a natural one. Possibly the crunch of a slender branch under a stealthy boot.

Yakima rose to his knees. Quietly, gritting his teeth, he racked a cartridge into the Yellowboy's action, then off-cocked the hammer. He rose to his feet and moved, keeping very low, to a mesquite several yards ahead.

He looked around.

Seeing nothing, hearing no more sounds but desert birds piping in the spikes and thorns around him, he moved around the mesquite and traced a meandering course toward the dyke dead ahead of him. The climbing, intensifying morning sun sucked up shadows along the rocky formation's left side, casting the outcropping in a harsh, flame-colored glare and seemingly pulling it back away from the Apache Springs lawman, obscuring it with the optical illusion of increased distance.

Yakima stepped around the left side of a one-armed saguaro. A man stood twenty feet away from him, on the other side of an oblong clearing. Damaso Guzman's tall, rangy figure was clad in leather and deerskin, a filthy red bandanna knotted around his neck. The dragon on Guzman's forehead breathed fire just above the bridge of his broad, dark nose and beneath the wide brim of his ragged black opera hat sporting a single hawk feather.

The Mexican smiled a toothy grin, seedy eyes slitting.

Yakima jerked back behind the saguaro as the Mexican's rifle spat smoke and orange flames. The bullet screeched over Yakima's left shoulder and sang off a rock behind him. Two more bullets sailed toward him, one plunking dully into the far side of the saguaro.

Before the report of the third shot had stopped echoing, Yakima stepped out to the right side of the saguaro and cut loose with the Yellowboy, firing from his hip. One, two, three times he pulled the trigger, quickly and smoothly working the cocking lever. The Mexican stumbled back and ran, returning fire with his carbine.

Yakima's bullets plumed rocks and gravel around the Mexican's high-heeled Sonora boots with their large, silver spurs until the fourth shot smacked the tall, rangy Mex's right leg out from beneath him. Guzman dropped to his knees with a curse, grabbing his right thigh.

Cursing, the Mexican scrambled away, crawling desperately, kicking up dust, toward a boulder as Yakima emptied the Yellowboy at him. More dirt and gravel hammered the desert around where Guzman heaved himself to his feet and flung himself headlong behind a boulder, cursing loudly in Spanish.

Hot lead tore a chunk out of Yakima's side a quarter-second before he heard a man's wild laughter and the screeching and bellowing of what sounded like a Spencer carbine—a big caliber popper, maybe a .50 or .56 caliber. The pain of the bullet searing his side, just above his cartridge belt, Yakima threw himself left and down behind the saguaro.

More of those big-caliber bullets tore up the ground around him. He crawled out away from the direction the shots were coming from, away from the saguaro, keeping the big cactus between him and his would-be killer.

He dropped the empty Yellowboy, drew his stag-gripped Army Colt, and rolled behind a tuft of grease-wood and a low, cracked rock close beside it.

More bullets came, hammering the rock, peppering Yakima with the sharp rock shards.

The Spencer fell silent.

Gritting his teeth against the pain in his side, leaning the back of his head against the rock, Yakima rolled onto his left shoulder and glanced quickly around the rock's right side. Mankiller was striding toward him, just then pausing to carefully set the empty Spencer on the ground near his left boot.

He was partly concealed by a mesquite, its branches sagging under the weight of beans. Through the long slender leaves of the tree, Yakima could see the big, broad-shouldered man striding toward him, crouched low, head down, his deep-copper face mostly concealed by the broad brim of his bullet-shaped hat.

Yakima could see the dark eyes staring up at him from beneath the very edge of the hat. An animal hide pouch, maybe a tobacco or a medicine pouch, dangled from a braided rawhide thong from around his thick neck. Mankiller was a big man, as tall as Yakima, but thicker through the belly, beefier, his face broad and savage, his thin-lipped mouth set cruelly below his broad, belligerent nose. Long black hair hung down past his shoulders.

Yakima jerked up his Colt. Mankiller stepped behind the mesquite's trunk, and the two shots Yakima triggered flew wild. The reverberations of the second shot were still echoing when Mankiller bounded back out from behind the tree, triggering his own six-shooter toward Yakima as he ran from Yakima's left to his right, weaving between creosote shrubs and ocotillos, his long hair dancing about his broad, thick shoulders. He moved like a big man, his gate lumbering, heavy-footed. Yakima could hear him grunting.

Crouched low, wincing against the bullets peppering the ground and air around him, Yakima returned fire, the Colt bucking wildly as he tracked the big figure clad in dark denims, a calico shirt, and high-topped, mule-eared boots racing through the chaparral in a broad semi-circle around him.

Through his own wafting gray powder smoke, Yakima saw Mankiller go down. He couldn't tell if the man had gone to ground intentionally or if he'd bought one of the .44 rounds Yakima had triggered.

Quickly, Yakima raised the Colt's barrel. He flicked

open the loading gate and turned the wheel quickly, shaking out the spent cartridges. He replaced them with those on his cartridge belt, clicked the gate back into place, and spun the cylinder.

He aimed the gun straight out before him. He was breathing hard from pain and anxiety, expecting to see the big Apache half-breed bearing down on him with Mankiller's own six-shooter.

Yakima squinted one eye down the Colt's barrel, ready to plant a bead on the Indian's thick figure. He slid the gun left, then right. He turned his head to peer behind him then swung it forward again.

No sign of the big Indian.

What the hell?

Something clicked to Yakima's right. He jerked the Colt in that direction, and fired, instantly realizing that he'd been tricked. Mankiller had thrown a rock to distract him.

4

A roaring howl rose from Yakima's far right.

Mankiller grinned from over the top of the earth mounded up around the base of a large saguaro, extending his own Colt toward Yakima.

Shit!

As smoke and flames lapped from the Indian's six-shooter, Yakima leaped up and hurled himself backward over his rock—an acrobatic move spurred by the threat of instant peril. Mankiller hadn't expected a man Yakima's size to move that fast. Yakima himself hadn't. The bullet slammed into the face of the rock where Yakima had been crouched only a quarter-second before.

Yakima extended his .44 over the top of the rock, quickly lined up the sights on the big dark face glowering from over the mounded earth, and fired. Mankiller's head drew back and down, obscured by Yakima's and the

Indian's own smoke haze.

Yakima clicked the gun's hammer back and aimed through the smoke, waiting.

Waiting.

No movement over there.

Silence.

The rotten egg smell of cordite hung heavy in the still, hot desert air. The wound in Yakima's side burned and throbbed like a son of a bitch. The pain made it hard to stay focused. It made him feel queasy, his knees weak.

Yakima triggered another shot, blowing up gravel from near the saguaro's base. Still, nothing moved. No sounds.

Slowly, keeping the cocked Colt extended toward the mound of earth, Yakima gained his feet. He brushed his left hand across his side. It came away bloody. He looked down. His shirt and coat were bloody. He'd taken a hot one, all right. He couldn't tell how bad it was. It hurt like hell, but they all hurt like hell, the bad as well as the not-so-bad ones.

He moved slowly forward, squeezing the cocked Colt in his right hand. Apprehension drew his muscles taut. A trickster, Mankiller might be playing possum. But as Yakima stepped past the saguaro, he eased the tension in his trigger finger.

If Mankiller was playing possum, he was one hell

of an actor.

The Indian lay stretched out on the ground about six feet beyond the saguaro. His arms were raised as though in surrender, the Colt still in his right hand, the hammer down. His legs were spread wide. He stared up at the sky. At least one eye stared skyward. The other had been blown to tomato paste. The same bullet had obviously blown out the back of his head, for a good deal of blood and white bone matter pillowed his head and stained his long, coal-black hair fanned out beneath him.

A sound rose from behind Yakima. He swung around heavily, the pain making him weak and dizzy. He raised the Colt again. He saw nothing. Scraping thuds and grunts sounded in the desert to the southeast, toward the dyke, which was brassy with sunlight now.

Yakima moved forward. As he did, he removed a handkerchief from his back pocket, wadded it, and pressed it taut against the wound to stem the blood flow. The throbbing pain made him shiver. As the grunts and scraping sounds continued issuing from somewhere ahead, he quickened his pace.

When he'd strode maybe twenty yards, weaving through the chaparral, he saw Guzman staggering through the desert, dragging one leg, moving away from Yakima. Beyond the Mexican, two horses stood tied to the short, skeletal branches of a fallen tree. Yakima strode forward. Hearing him, Guzman stopped, snaked a pistol around his body, and snapped off a shot toward Yakima.

The man was staggering, holding the pistol unsteadily, and the bullet flew wide. He turned his head forward and continued dragging his wounded leg toward the horses.

Yakima kept walking, raising his Colt. "You ain't gonna make it, Domaso!"

Again, Guzman snaked the pistol around his body and snapped another shot toward Yakima—or within two dozen yards of him, anyway. The wild round plunked into a saguaro far to Yakima's right.

Yakima aimed the Colt and blew the Mexican's other leg out from under him. Guzman yelped and fell in a heap.

Yakima walked up to where the man lay writhing. He'd dropped his pistol and was clutching at both bullet-torn legs. The man's left leg was nearly covered in blood. The right leg was well on its way toward the same condition. The bullet in his left leg had chewed through an artery. With no sawbones near, he'd be saddling a golden cloud soon.

"You ain't gonna make it," Yakima repeated.

Guzman lay belly down. He lifted his head and gave an agonized wail of pain before flopping over onto his back. He glared up at the man who'd shot him.

He had an oddly moon-shaped face free of hair except a sparse, dark-brown mustache mantling his upper lip. His nose was short and broad, his dark eyes set wide beneath a single, bushy brow. The fire-breathing dragon took up most of his broad, high forehead, beneath a cap of tightly curled, dark-brown hair caked with adobe-colored dust.

Now Guzman lifted his ugly head up off the ground, jutting his weak chin at Yakima. It was like being threatened by an infant's fist. The Mexican cut loose with a wild string of Spanish only half of which Yakima could understand and which dealt with Yakima's questionable bloodline and several other things too personal to mention. By the time the Mexican was finished, he'd spent himself; spittle frothed on his thick, liver-colored lips.

He sagged back against the ground.

"As I was sayin'," Yakima said, "you ain't gonna make it. Why did Mankiller stick that knife in Barnes's back?"

"Go to the devil, you Indio bastardo!"

"Joke's on you, Domaso," Yakima said. "The way you're bleedin' out, you're almost there."

Guzman gave a hideous laugh though no humor reached his flattening gaze. "The joke's on you, Indio lawman. The joke's on *you*!"

That last took the last bit of venom out of the dying man. His body convulsed then relaxed. He gave a ragged sigh. His muddy eyes rolled up in his head and he gave one more small spasm and a fart, and lay still.

Yakima scowled down at him. "What the hell'd you mean by that?"

***

Julia Taggart strode down the Conquistador Inn's third floor hall, quiet this early in the morning, and stopped at a door at the hall's far end. She drew a calming breath and raised her hand. She hesitated, chewing her lower lip, pensive, then went ahead and tapped on the door.

"Pa," she said, leaning close to the door, keeping her voice down in deference to the hour. "It's Julia. A word, please?"

No response.

She frowned. The sun was up, which meant it was likely going on eight o'clock. She knew her father to be an early riser. At least, he usually rose early when he was at their sprawling house near the headquarters of his gold mine, the Conquistador. He often saw his regular trips to town as sojourns from the isolation of his life in the Sierra Estrada, and often slept in a little later than usual after indulging his taste for poker and whiskey with his business associates.

He was in town now, staying in his usual suite at the hotel, for the celebration of the railroad's arrival, so it was more than possible he'd enjoyed himself even more than usual last night, and was sleeping off a hangover. Julia had seen him in the Puma Den downstairs, the Conquistador's lavish gambling parlor, with two territorial senators and men from the Central Arizona Railroad's Board of Directors. Hugh Kosgrove had been throwing back his favored Scotch whiskey, and, rosy-cheeked and glassy-eyed, not to mention typically loud, he'd obviously been feeling no pain.

Julia knocked again, louder. She didn't care how much pain the old goat was feeling. She needed to talk to him, and she wasn't going to wait.

"Pa?" she said through the upper panel. "It's Julia. I'd like..." She tried the knob and was surprised to hear the latching bolt click back into the door.

She drew it open and stepped inside, looking around. "Pa?"

She was in the parlor/office area of his two-room suite. No lamps were lit and the velveteen curtains were closed against the weak morning sunlight. On the book case to Julia's left, a silver kitchen tray held a silver coffee server and two china cups and saucers. There were also two still-steaming sweet rolls in a basket. The coffee and the sweet rolls flavored the air enticingly, making Julia realize how hungry she was.

When he was staying at the Conquistador, Hugh Kosgrove always had the breakfast cook bring him coffee and a roll. Apparently, this morning, old Kosgrove had not been ready to receive the tray, so the cook, Charlie Wentz, had left the tray where Julia's father would find it once he arose.

Voices issuing from the partially open door in the wall to Julia's left clarified things. She heard her father's low voice, speaking softly. It was followed by a female voice. A girl's voice. A voice that Julia recognized. Behind that partly open door, Kosgrove gave a long, weary sigh. The girl giggled.

Julia strode across the room and paused at the door, fingering the knob, hesitating. Finally, she glanced into the room briefly, quickly turning away but not before the damage had been done. In that one-second glance, she'd seen her father sitting on the edge of his bed, his stubby, heavy-bellied body clad in absolutely nothing. A naked young doxie—Nellie Pearl—knelt between his spread knees.

Hugh Kosgrove sagged back toward the bed, propped on his locked arms, chin tipped toward the bed's spruce green canopy, a dreamy smile on his goatish old face. The doxie raised and lowered her head, her hair hanging down over both cheeks.

Anger flaming inside Julia, she turned her head back for another glaring look into the room, and said, "Really, Pa? *Nellie?*" She gave a deep groan of disdain and slammed the door.

"Julia!" he exclaimed in his shrill, raspy voice that still owned a little of his native Irish brogue. "What on

God's green—"

Behind the door, the doxie, Nellie Pearl, gave a thick laugh. Julia heard the bed creak and sigh as Hugh Kosgrove heaved his bullet-shaped bulk up and then stomped around the room, likely gathering his clothes.

Smiling with a devilish but deserved satisfaction—at least deserved to her way of thinking—Julia walked back over to the server, poured herself a cup of coffee, and strode over to a window on the room's far side, near the potbelly stove. Her father's desk was on the opposite side of the room from the bedroom, under the head of a large elk he shot himself on the Mogollon Rim, on one of his storied hunting expeditions with business associates which usually included a few territorial senators, an attorney general or two, and sometimes even a governor.

While her father continued cursing and stumbling around in the bedroom, Julia opened the drapes so she could stare out over the smoky rooftops toward the west, toward where the shiny new rails curved across the plain. The sun was well on the rise, turning saffron the plain below the plateau on which Apache Springs sprawled, on the first rise of the Sierra Estrada.

Behind Julia, the bedroom door opened. Julia turned to see Nellie step out and close the door behind her. Her slender, snow-white body was clad in only several coils of faux pearls. Her breasts were hardly larger than mosquito bites. The pretty, blue-eyed dove pulled a thin chemise down over her head then tossed her thick, blonde hair back behind her shoulders and glanced sheepishly toward Julia.

Her pale cheeks were as red as roses.

"He paid me extra, Miss Julia!" The girl shrugged, hurried to the door, opened it, and cast one more obsequious glance at Julia. She stepped into the hall then drew the door quietly closed behind her.

The bedroom came open again and the penguin-like Hugh Kosgrove stepped through the door belly-first, his fleshy face as red as Nellie's had been. His bullet-shaped head owned a short cap of close-cropped, silver hair, and long silver muttonchops framed his swarthy face. He wore his royal red bathrobe, and he was tying the drawstring around his considerable girth, half of an unlit stogie protruding from a corner of his mouth. His spindly legs were clad in silk longhandles. Wool-lined, elk skin slippers adorned his small, white feet.

"Well, that was one hell of a rude interruption!" he intoned, waddling across the room to the serving tray. "I sent you girls to the best schools in the country, and you still got the manners of waterfront orphans."

"Did you ask her how old she is?"

"I don't care how old they are!" Kosgrove spat out, glowering incredulously at his oldest daughter regarding him with the brightly cajoling eyes of a schoolmarm.

"She's not yet seventeen!"

"Really?" Kosgrove poured himself a cup of coffee, wagging his head and smiling his amazement. "Could have fooled me." He chuckled, dropped his cigar into a pocket of his robe, and lifted the coffee to his lips.

"You're disgusting."

Kosgrove sipped his coffee, swallowed, and hiked a shoulder. "I'm a man." He moved toward the sofa running along the wall dividing the bedroom from the parlor/office part of the suite.

"One and the same—is that it?"

"You don't think so?"

"I'm sorry to say, I do." Julia's mood turned grim as she thought of Yakima Henry and her younger sister, Emma.

"You know—I think John Clare might be a little above the norm." Kosgrove sat on the couch and, leaning forward, elbows on his knees, held the cup to his lips with both of his small, thick hands. He wore a gold ring on his right pinky, which he extended with improbable daintiness as he sipped. Hugh Kosgrove was many things, but he was not a dainty man. "I hope you're taking his fawning seriously."

John Clare Hopkins was a business associate of Kosgrove's—a dapper, handsome Englishman in his thirties who had so much family money that he could travel around the world amusing himself by speculating in various business ventures, including gold mines and railroads and such. He'd helped Hugh out of a tight spot when the older man had gotten himself in dire financial straits with some risky investments.

Hopkins seemed to like Hugh immensely. He resided here in Apache Springs for what seemed the sole purpose of drinking and carousing and gambling with Julia's adventurous and charismatic father. He owned interests in several businesses, including the Conquistador Hotel as well as the mine, but Julia was still under the impression that John Clare Hopkins remained here in this relative jerkwater because he so enjoyed her father. In fact, he fawned over the shorter, older, louder man like the adoring son Hugh had never had.

Ignoring her father's comment concerning the attentions Hopkins also paid Julia, she changed the subject to the one she'd come here for: "What do you have on Yakima Henry?"

45

5

"How do you know about that?" Hugh Kosgrove asked.

"I just do. What is it? What's the big secret?"

Kosgrove took another sip of his coffee then sank back in the sofa. He set the coffee on a knee. "He killed a deputy marshal up in Kansas."

"Why?"

"Does it matter?"

"It might."

"All that matters is he killed a federal lawman, Julia. He has a federal warrant as well as a two-thousand-dollar bounty on his head." Kosgrove scowled, shook his red-faced head with his red jowls and piercing blue eyes. "Why are we talking about him? You can't have feelings for that man, Julia. You can't!"

Looking miserable, Kosgrove set his coffee on the table before him, rose, and ambled over to where his daughter stood in front of the window. She was an inch or two taller than her father, though he was a good bit thicker and wider. He reached up and gently caressed her cheek with the back of his plump, beringed hand.

"Julia, look at you. You're a beautiful woman. The spitting image of your dear ma. You can have any man you want!"

Gazing down at the ugly little man with the fiery Irish gaze, Julia gave an ironic curl of her mouth. Hugh of course didn't recognize the irony in the fact that Julia's mother had married him, the brass Irish penguin, despite that she probably had the pick of several litters herself. But, then, of course Hugh didn't see Yakima Henry as a handsome man. He saw only his red skin. He saw a savage. When he imagined his daughter and Yakima together, he likely pictured several half-breed children running around, yipping like coyotes.

Julia suppressed another smile. For some reason, the image amused her. She thought that she could be very happy bearing Yakima Henry's children. A whole litter of them. The idea of the big, half-wild man's seed taking root in her womb brought a flush to her face.

She turned to the window, giving her father her back.

Kosgrove placed a hand on her shoulder. "I have three words for you, my beauty: John Clare Hopkins."

"It's not that I'm not attracted to Mister Hopkins, Pa."

"What is it, then?"

Julia crossed her arms on her breasts that she felt coming alive with desire. "I love him, Pa."

"Well, that's just silly!" Kosgrove gave an angry wail and walked back over to the sofa and sank into it. He scrubbed a hand over his unshaven face and swollen jowls. "Lord in Heaven—what did I do to you two girls to treat me this way? First you marry a…a local lawman…"

"Lon was a good man, Pa!"

"Oh, hell—I know that. Yes, yes, Lon Taggart was a very good man. But he was a lawman, honey. He was never going to amount to much—may God rest his soul," Kosgrove added in his own obligatory nod to decorum.

Julia gave a frustrated groan and turned to face the old man, balling her fists at her sides. Before she could lash into him, professing the higher morality of character over money, her father continued with: "And then you fall for a *half-breed*. Another lawman! A *half-breed lawman* who killed a deputy U.S. marshal in Kansas! Not only that, but your sister has fallen for the same damn *rock-worshipper*!"

"Oh, Jesus!" Julia pressed her hands to her temples, feeling as though her head were about to explode. "I have to get out of here!"

Keeping her hands to her head, she made her way to the door.

"Honey, please!" her father called in wheedling tone behind her. "Listen to reason. It's a cold, hard world out there. You need the right man to take care of you!"

Julia fumbled the door open.

"John Clare Hopkins is the man for you, sweetheart!" Hugh Kosgrove yelled as she hurried into the hall and pulled the door closed behind her.

Placing a hand to her head again, Julia staggered as though drunk, running up against the wall opposite her father's room. Her head pounded, and her insides churned. Her father's voice echoed around inside her brain: "You need the right man to take care of you!"

Did she? Is that really what she needed? Did she need to be cared for more than loved?

She couldn't help agreeing with her father's exasperation at the fact of her and Emma having fallen in love with the same man. She'd been trying to push that unruly, prickly fact to the back of her mind, because it got in the way of her true feelings for Yakima, but now it was right there in front of her again, complicating her thoughts.

Again, she saw them in her imagination's overly keen eye—toiling together in his roughhewn bed in that humble adobe shack of his out in the Sierra Estrada.

"You all right, Miss Julia?"

She lowered her hand and was surprised to see another half-dressed young doxie moving toward her sleepily, her

49

hair in her eyes, her lampblack and rouge badly sleep-smeared. It was Candace Jo coming up from the kitchen with a steaming mug of coffee in her hands.

Julia feigned a smile. "Just a little too early after a long night is all."

The girl scrutinized Julia skeptically then smiled her gap-toothed smile and started to turn away.

"Hold on." Julia grabbed the girl's arm and turned her back toward her. Candace's left eye was slightly discolored. Julia brushed her thumb across the discoloration. "What happened here?"

"Oh, it's nothing."

"It isn't nothing," Julia said, her anger rising. "What happened, Candace? Who did this?"

"Ah, I don't wanna say, Miss Julia. Please, don't make me."

"*Who?*"

"Please, I…"

"Candace, you need to tell me. My clients know very well my rules. They know that if they step out of line, they will be cut off and barred from the premises!"

"He didn't mean nothin' by it."

"Who, Candace?" Julia asked again, firmly.

Candace gave a pained expression. "It was just one of the miners…you know…one of the boys who works for Mister Hamms out at the Periwinkle. I don't even know his name."

"Mister Hamms, huh? All right. I will have a talk with Mister Hamms."

"It's all right, Miss Julia. Really it is. The boy just got a little frustrated, is all. He'd had too much to drink."

"They can get frustrated all they want, but when they take it out on my girls, they get cut off."

Julia felt motherly toward the girls who worked in her and her father's employ. Pleasing men was a nasty business. It meant you had to submit to them, which was dangerous. Especially in the boom town Apache Springs had become. Julia didn't like running such a business, but if she didn't serve as madam to the young doxies here at the Conquistador, her father would only hire someone else—possibly someone who didn't have Julia's concern and well-being for the girls foremost in her mind.

Besides, the eight girls who worked for her here at the hotel had become her family, of sorts. She felt closer to them than she did in many ways to her own sister and even her father. She was like an older sister to her covey of doves, though some were nearly as old as she was at twenty-eight.

"Take a hot bath," Julia told Candace. "And remember—if anyone gets rough with you, you come and see me right away. You don't have to stand for that, Candace. I won't have you standing for it. Understand?"

"Yes, ma'am."

"Run along."

The girl hurried off down the hall in her bare feet, pink chemise, and white pantaloons.

Julia drew a deep breath and closed her eyes, trying to calm herself. What a morning it had been so far. Not only was her mind in turmoil, but her body had been so ready for Yakima's big, masculine body earlier that she felt physically frustrated, as well, adding to her general malaise.

What she needed was a cup of coffee. She'd had only a few sips of her father's.

She strode on down the hall then down the broad staircase to the first story where the steady hum of conversation rose around her, as did the clinking of forks on plates. She was pleased to see that the large main saloon hall on both sides of the big, horseshoe-shaped bar were occupied by breakfasting businessmen and traveling drummers.

Several men in business suits passed Julia on the stairs as they returned to their upstairs rooms, nodding to her, smiling, pinching the brims of their bowler hats, letting their furtive eyes linger over her figure. She was well aware that her body was pleasing to men.

She'd known that for a long time, for she'd matured early, so she'd learned long ago how to parry such attentions. She'd grown up sheltered out at the Conquistador mine, in her father's sprawling Spanish-style casa, but he'd sent her to finishing school for several years back east. He'd sent Emma, as well, though due to poor grades and innate rebelliousness, Julia's younger sister had been kicked out and sent home. Now Emma rode around the desert on green-broke stallions—a green-broke girl riding broom-tailed cayuses hither and yon, not a care in the world, nor a responsibility. She was a horseback, flaxen-haired siren.

A seductress of men as untamed and untamable as Emma herself was...

Julia flared a nostril in general annoyance at her sister. She stepped up to the bar and asked the morning barman, Ivor Ingersoll, for a cup of coffee. Ingersoll had just set three coffees on the tray of one of the serving girls, and added a jigger of brandy to each.

"That's a good idea," Julia said. "Why don't you pay mine the same compliment?"

"All right." Ingersoll turned away to pour coffee from a large urn on the backbar. He cast Julia a smile over his shoulder. "Long night, Miss Julia?"

Julia flushed. More like a hard morning, for she hadn't had her ashes hauled by the man she'd wanted to haul them. She wondered if a man could read sexual frustration in a woman's face.

"You could say that," was all she muttered as the barman set the china cup of coffee onto a saucer before her, and splashed Spanish brandy into it.

"Now, that's what the doctor ordered!"

The voice had come from behind her, rising above the general hum of the morning diners. Julia looked over her shoulder to see none other than John Clare Hopkins striding up behind her, smiling in his oily way, long dark lashes dropping down over his confident—some might even say arrogant—brown eyes.

"Indeed." Julia smiled at the tall, handsome man in his customary, tailor-made three-piece suit, celluloid collar, and black foulard tie. "Good morning, John. How are you?"

"Absolutely splendid. The bed in my room must have been made by God himself. I always sleep so well when I stay here at the Conquistador." Indeed, the English investor stayed at the Conquistador whenever he was in Apache Springs, and he'd been here for quite a while now—several months. That was a good bit of time for a man so moneyed, adventurous, and fiddle-footed. "The place is so well run. Your people see to my every need."

"Well, that's what we're here for," Julia said, smiling as she sipped her coffee. She glanced behind him. He'd come from a table set against the wall, beneath the snarling head of a grizzly and to the right of a cabinet clock. Three other men encircled the table, which surprised Julia somewhat. John Clare Hopkins was usually a solitary breakfaster.

Turning his handsome head, Hopkins followed her gaze. "Ah—yes. You see I have company. Why don't you step over and meet the horde?"

"The horde?"

"Yes, that's what I call them. The Wild Limey Horde." Hopkins threw his head back and laughed beneath his thick brown mustache as he led Julia over to the table at which four other men sat, their eyes now scouring Julia with customary male interest, fawning smiles pulling at their mouths.

Formally, Hopkins dipped his chin, rose up and down on the heels of his polished half boots, and said, "Miss Julia Taggart, won't you meet my younger brother, Ferrell Hopkins?"

The younger Hopkins smiled and gave a cordial bow over his empty breakfast platter and coffee cup. He was a redhead, and more delicately structured than John Clare, but Julia could see a definite family resemblance in the features and builds of the two Hopkins men.

"Beside him there," continued the older Hopkins, going around the table clockwise, "is our friend the Irishman Liam Peale. The tall rascal with the ridiculous mustachios is the venerable Brian McKenzie—a vile-tempered Scott!" he added behind his hand to Julia in a feigned whisper.

The others chuckled while McKenzie grinned and raised a shot glass to his mouth, which was, indeed, mantled with a most impressive, coal-black mustache.

Hopkins said, "Completing this chummy and virile quartet is last but not least H. Bennett "Milo" Cartwright. Don't ask me where the Milo came from, but that is what everyone calls him so Milo it is, indeed."

"Miss Taggart," said Cartwright with a cordial nod of his own. "It is my deepest pleasure." He sat nearest Julia—close enough, in fact, to take her hand in his own pale one, lift it to his mouth, and pressed his lips to it. The moistness of his mouth made Julia recoil inwardly slightly, but she smiled and, removing her hand from Cartwright's, said, "Why, thank you, sir." With a smiling, sidelong glance up at John Clare Hopkins, she said, "But it's Mrs. Taggart. I'm a widow."

"Oh, what a shame!" said the Scott, McKenzie, furling his heavy black brows. "And such a young widow, at that." His large dark eyes drifted to her bodice.

"Her husband was the town marshal of Apache Springs," Hopkins explained to his friends. "He was killed...as I understand...by one of the nastiest pack of curly wolves the American frontier has ever seen."

Julia found something somewhat discomfiting, if not vaguely jeering, in the man's tone. In fact, she found a similar quality to the obsequious gazes of the other men at the table—a vague mockery perhaps of not only her but her deceased husband and the entire frontier West, which they seemed to regard with the mock seriousness of men who saw the world as merely a series of playgrounds provided for their amusement and entertainment.

She might have merely been feeling a little thin-skinned after her experience—or lack thereof—with Yakima earlier, followed so closely by the nearly as frustrating conversation with her badgering, tyrannical father. Be that as it may, she wanted very much only to return to the bar and to her spiced coffee, which she so desperately needed right now.

Ignoring Hopkins' last comment and wanting merely to end the conversation with a polite query, Julia beamed her winning, businesswoman's smile, and asked, "So, what, gentlemen, brings you all to Apache Springs?" She glanced at Hopkins standing beside her. "Don't tell me you've all come so far to join the gold-seekers?"

A curious flush touched John Clare Hopkins's cheeks. A similar one found its way into the finer, paler face of his smaller, younger, less handsome brother, who smiled stiffly and raised his own shot glass to his mouth. The other men glanced at each other, vaguely duplicitous.

"Friendship," John Clare Hopkins said, a little more loudly than was necessary. "Just friendship...mainly. But, of course, we're all businessmen here, and that means we're always on the scout for investment opportunities."

"I see," Julia said, feeling a little baffled by the men's stiff reactions to her question. She herself was too distracted by her own problems to probe any further. By way of politely breaking off the conversation, she said, "Allow me to welcome you to Apache Springs in general and to my father's grand hotel, the Conquistador Inn. I do hope your stay here will be comfortable and rewarding, and if there's anything I can do to help in that regard, please let me know. I'm almost always on the premises, mostly running around like a chicken with my head cut off!"

She feigned a laugh at the tedious joke and began to turn back to the bar. "Now, if you'll excuse me..."

"Thank you, Miss Taggart," intoned Ferrell Hopkins over the rim of his half-filled shot glass.

"Nice to meet you, Miss Taggart," said the man called Cartwright.

The other two men nodded at her in parting. As she headed back toward the bar, John Clare Hopkins followed her closely, gently closing his hand around her arm, stopping her before she could reach her longed-for coffee and brandy.

"Uh...Julia?" he said, hesitating and fashioning an unctuous smile. "I was wondering if you'd consider having dinner with me this evening. Perhaps drinks with me and the others"—he canted his head toward his brother and friends and/or business associates— "and then dinner… just the two of us?"

His smile broadened with gentle beseeching.

"Oh." Julia wasn't sure what to say. She was really in no mood to be romanced by anyone other than…

Just then she saw him out one of the saloon's two large front windows—Yakima Henry riding an unfamiliar horse into Julia's view, from her right. He rode slumped a little in his saddle, pressing his gloved left hand against what appeared a bloody wound in his left side. He rode on the far side of the newly laid tracks, obscured by sunlit dust rising from the hooves and wheels of riders and wagons passing in both directions along the street.

Yakima was leading two horses by their bridle reins. A dead man lay belly down over the back of each saddled horse, though all Julia could see of the men was their legs and boots. Their arms and heads hung down the horses' far sides.

"Julia…?" Hopkins said, frowning at her with a vague annoyance.

"Oh, dear," she muttered, backing away from John Clare Hopksins. "I'm sorry, John. I'll have to give you my answer later!"

She swung around and hurried to the front door.

6

"Marshal!"

Galveston Penny came down off the jailhouse's front stoop and ran into the street, the finely churned powder of dust and horse apples wafting up around his ankles. He squinted against the midday sun as he gazed up at Yakima then looked past the half-breed lawman riding the young deputy's own horse, to the two dead men lying belly down over the saddles of the two horses in Yakima's pack string.

"Well, you got 'em both, I see," said young Penny. "Got 'em good. There any life left in either of 'em?"

Yakima swung down from the zebra dun's back. "Nope."

Galveston grabbed a bridle cheek strap and caressed the dun's snout with affection, smiling proudly. "How did old Zeb do? He do all right for you? He come up from

Texas with me—a gift from an old rancher I worked for. They said he was old and no good anymore, but he's been a right steady trail mount for me."

Yakima glanced from Galveston to the older horse, who'd left him high and dry after Mankiller and Guzman had opened up on him. After the marshal had killed both killers, he'd looked around for the horse, but it had disappeared, likely frightened off by the gunfire. It had reappeared behind him as he was riding one of the two dead men's horses back in the direction of Apache Springs...and oats, hay, and water.

The horse had looked a little sheepish, following along from about thirty yards back, keeping its head down, ears pinned back. Rather than ride double with a dead man, Yakima had mounted the zebra and rode it back to town.

Now he gave an indifferent grunt as, pressing his left hand against the bullet wound in his left side, he stepped around the kid and dropped to his knees before the stock trough fronting the jail office. As per his morning duties, Galveston had filled the trough with fresh water only a couple of hours ago. Yakima brushed his hat off, letting it tumble into the dirt, and plunged his head into the lukewarm water, taking a long drink as he did.

He lifted his head from the tank and shook it, whipping his long hair out around him, water flying everywhere.

"You're hit."

Yakima looked at the badly worn boots in the dirt to his left and trailed his eyes up the long, skinny, broadcloth-clad legs and lean waist and chest to the concerned eyes of young Penny scowling down at the bloody stain in his side.

"Take the fresh beef over to the undertaker, will you?"

"You best have the doc look at that."

"Sutton's got his hands full."

"Still, that don't look too good. I'd best…"

"You'd best take these two bushwhackers over to the undertaker's and—"

"Yakima!" This time it was a woman's voice.

Yakima turned to see Julia making her way over from the Conquistador on the other side of the street and to the west a couple of blocks. She angled toward him, holding the skirts of her expensive, low-cut gown above her side-button shoes, negotiating the heavy mid-day traffic. She narrowed her eyes against the roiling dust, coughing.

When a small ore wagon pulled by two jackasses passed before her, giving her an opening to Yakima's side of the street, she hurried up to where the lawman was rising from the dirt and saying, "This day just keeps bunchin' up on me." He looked at the young string-bean deputy standing beside him, staring at the hole in the lawman's side. "Galveston, what did I just tell you to do?"

"S-Sorry, Marshal!" Galveston gathered up the

pack horse's reins, swung up onto his dun's back, and booted it up the street, tugging the two pack horses along behind him.

Julia stopped before Yakima, glowering down at his side. "How bad?"

"Hell, I—"

"I know, I know. You've cut yourself worse shaving. I highly doubt that. Let's get you over to Doc Sutton's."

Yakima shook his head. "Doc's got his hands full with the Rio Grande Kid and the stage passengers. He doesn't got time for a little bullet burn."

Julia gazed pleadingly into his eyes. "Let me take a look at it."

"No." Yakima turned away, mounted the brush-roofed gallery fronting the adobe brick jailhouse and kicked open the partly open door, glad to see the four cells lined up along the back wall empty. Galveston had likely collected the fines of the drunks he'd hauled in last night, and let them go. Good. Yakima wanted a little peace and quiet and a cup of coffee. Later, he'd head over to the doctor's place to check on the Rio Grande Kid.

He grabbed a blue-speckled pan and a washcloth off the copper-topped wash stand, walked back out onto the gallery, and grunted in frustration to see Julia standing before him, just outside the door. He dunked the pan in the water barrel on the stoop's left side then turned and tramped back into the office.

He set the pan on the desk which faced out from the left wall, flanked by a map of Arizona Territory as well as the thirty-eight starred red-white-and-blue. The office remained pretty much as Julia's dead husband, Marshal Lon Taggart, had left it when he'd been killed by outlaws before Julia and Yakima's own eyes, the half-breed having been locked up at the time that viciousness had occurred.

Yakima sagged into the swivel Windsor chair behind the desk, opened the desk's bottom drawer, and pulled out a whiskey bottle.

In the periphery of his vision, he watched Julia enter the office stiffly, hesitantly, and stop a few feet in front of the door. Yakima dumped a quarter of the whiskey into the water then soaked a wash cloth in the whiskey-laced water, and wrung it out with both hands.

"I talked to my father," Julia said, squeezing her hands together.

Yakima pulled his shirt out of his pants. He lifted the tail and peered under it at the bloody wound about six inches above his cartridge belt. He ripped the shirt open, laying his belly bare, then lifted the bottle to his lips, taking a healthy pull.

"I know all about the lawman in Kansas," Julia said, glancing at the hard, flat, copper slab of his belly.

Yakima took another long pull from the whiskey, set

the bottle down on the desk.

"I don't care," Julia said.

"Well, you should." Yakima dabbed the rag at the ragged tear in his flesh. The bullet had nipped him, digging about a half inch of flesh out of his side. He'd lost flesh in nearly the exact place before, and it had grown back. It would grow back again, adding another knotty lair to the twisted white scar.

Yakima sucked a sharp breath as he dabbed the rag at the wound again, a little harder this time, trying to mop up the half-dried blood masking a layer of gooier stuff.

Julia walked quickly around the desk. "Here—let me!"

"*No!*" His voice thundered around the small, adobe-walled, earthen-floored office.

She withdrew, stomped a foot in frustration, and gave her back to Yakima, crossing her arms on her breasts and gazing down at the floor.

Yakima wrung the bloody rag out in the now-bloody water and continued working on the wound, taking another sip of the whiskey, not wanting to get drunk because he knew what often happened when he over-indulged—his wolf would break its leash and run wild, howling—but wanting only to dull the pain. He wished Julia would leave. She wasn't helping his agony any. She aggravated it.

He needed to pull his picket pin. This couldn't be

a permanent home for him. He should have known that. A man with his violent past could never have a permanent home. He could never get this involved. Fall in love with another woman.

Well, he knew it well enough now...

Julia turned around to face him again. Her cheeks were touched with red and one eye was slightly crossed in barely contained anger. "Why is Emma always riding into the desert and staying out there for days?"

Yakima didn't say anything. He continued dabbing at the wound.

She tapped a foot on the floor. "Is she meeting you at the old rattlesnake nest you have out there in the Javelina Bluffs?"

"Yes," he said, the lie biting at him even more painfully now than the bullet burn. At least, he hadn't met Emma out there recently. He used to meet her out there, but he hadn't met her since he'd fallen in love with Julia several months ago now. "I'm sorry, Julia. I really am. I just couldn't help myself."

Fury sparked in her eyes. She lunged forward, pulling her right fist back behind her. Crouching, she heaved the fist forward and slammed it into Yakima's left side—right smack dab in the dead center of his bullet burn. She gave an enraged wail and said, "*There!* Think about that the next time you meet that desert whore of yours!"

She wheeled and strode, chin up, toward the door. She stopped with a gasp when a stocky figure shadowed the open doorway.

"Now, that's what I like to see!" Hugh Kosgrove threw his head back, slitting his blue eyes as he laughed his cackling, raspy laugh, his ruddy cheeks turning bright red. He held a half-smoked stogie between the index finger and thumb of his right hand, and the smoke was perfuming the somewhat pent up air of the jail office.

"Pa!" Julia shrilled.

Kosgrove stepped back and to one side, throwing an arm down and out, making way for his enraged oldest daughter. Flushed with humiliation, Julia lunged forward again to stride on out the door, down the steps and into the street, heading back in the direction of the Conquistador.

Yakima had lurched forward out of his chair. He knelt on one knee, pressing his left hand and the wadded cloth to his wound, which felt as though it had just been doused with kerosene and set aflame. He could feel the bite of Julia's punch all the way to his toes and to the hair at the top of his head.

Chuckling his seedy laugh, Kosgrove strode into the office, puffing on the cigar. "I'll be damned if she finally didn't actually listen to her old man. This a red-letter day for me, Henry. A red-letter day. Hah!"

"Gotta admit," Yakima choked out, bowing his head as he continued pressing the cloth to the wound, grinding his molars, "she packs one hell of a punch. You teach her that?"

"Nah. Prob'ly Emma. I used to worry about Emma around my miners until one grabbed her tit one day and she dislocated his jaw. Haven't worried since!" Kosgrove laughed. He was leaning against the wall near the wash stand, facing Yakima and puffing the cigar, the expression of unabashed delight slow to fade from his features. "I been worried about Julia around the drunken jakes at the hotel, but now I see I don't need to worry about her anymore, either. How you feelin'?"

"I've felt better."

"She couldn't have hit you that hard!"

"She smacked me where a bullet kissed me about an hour ago."

"Oh, lordy—now, I'm even more impressed. She knows right where to land a punch!"

Yakima scowled up at the fat little, red-faced Irishman all decked out in his three-piece, dark-green walrus suit with a metallic brown waistcoat and glistening gold watch chain and claw-hammer coat. He came complete with a bowler hat the same brown as the vest. "You have every right to be impressed, Kosgrove," the lawman said. "Quite a gal, quite a gal. Any father would be right proud to have sired such a pole-cat. But I'd admire like hell if you'd take your delight and delight in it elsewhere. I'd like to caterwaul in private."

"She's not the daughter I came over here for. I didn't know Julia was over here."

Yakima drew a breath and managed to gather enough strength to lift himself up off the floor and settle back into his chair. "Oh?" he said tightly, the pain slow to give ground. "Well, then...to what...do I owe the privilege?" He took a quick swig from the bottle, then another.

Kosgrove studied him through the smoke puffing in front of his face as he took several more deep drags off the stogie. "What happened?"

Yakima drew a breath. "Huh?"

"Who shot you, Henry? I believe I saw you ride in earlier with a couple of racks of fresh meat strapped to a couple of horses. I take it you're not market hunting these days...?"

"No, that was human beef. Good eye, Kosgrove." Yakima turned to him sidelong, relieved to note a slight easing of the pain in his side. "Gabrielle Mankiller and Domaso Guzman stuck a pig sticker in the back of Julian Barnes."

"Oh?"

"Ain't that's somethin'?" Yakima took another pull off the bottle. The whiskey filed a little sharpness from the bite in his side.

"It is somethin'," Kosgrove said, now standing with his thumbs hooked in the pockets of his waistcoat, regarding Yakima darkly from the shadows just inside the door, silhouetted by the bright sunlight pouring down behind his stocky, portly, garishly clad figure.

Yakima dipped the cloth in the water bowl again. "I wonder why those two would go after Barnes. Doesn't seem like their style—to go after an important man like that…in a *whorehouse*…just for what they could find in his pockets. They must have figured on a larger payout elsewhere." He slid a dubious eye toward the wealthy businessman once more. "Wouldn't you think so?"

The Irish walrus sounded indignant as he puffed up his chest and said, "What are you saying?"

"I'm not sure what I'm sayin'." Yakima wrung out the cloth. "Didn't he hornswoggle you out of a tidy sum awhile back?"

"Huh?"

"I heard from somebody…I forget who…that you and Barnes were in business together…till you had a falling out over money. They said he tricked you into making a shaky investment in a mine or some such…that he knew it was tricky…and that you ended up holding an empty sack while he came out flusher than before he went in. You didn't lose all that much in the deal, overall, but it piss-burned you because he made you look stupid. That have any truth in it or am I blowing hot air?"

"If you're suggesting I sicced those two pole-cats on Barnes, you're blowing hot air. If I wanted Barnes dead, I'd hire better men than those two scurvy dogs, and he'd be dead. Believe me."

"All right."

"Why is my daughter spending so much time out in the desert?"

Ah, Yakima thought. Now we get down to what lured him over to the wrong side of the tracks.

7

"Oh, hell." Yakima took another pull from the bottle.

"Tell me, dammit." Kosgrove took two waddling steps forward, moving into the light from a window near Yakima's desk, his blue eyes glinting with anger, his puffy cheeks like two red apples. "What's going on out there? She's gone more than she's home. At first, I thought she was spending time in town with Julia, but Julia put the kibosh to that notion."

Yakima dabbed at the wound, which Julia had opened up again, bless her heart. Somewhere in the back of his mind, he enjoyed the pain. It took his mind off his mental misery over having lost another chance to find love, to find a place to settle down finally, a place to grow old in, to die in. A cemetery plot beside a woman he'd spent thirty or forty years with…

"How the hell would I know?"

"Julia thinks you know."

"Yes, she does."

"Stop runnin' me around the Joshua tree, dammit! What is my daughter doing out there? Is she keeping house with you...in that old shack of yours?"

"No."

"What, then?"

Yakima looked at the man. He studied him critically. He wanted to tell him that Emma was spending most of her time out in the desert watching over the old church in the mysterious canyon, to keep anyone from looting the treasure the ancient church contained, but he couldn't do it. Part of him had suspected that old Kosgrove himself knew about it, and was biding his time, planning on ransacking it soon.

But now Yakima knew that wasn't true. Kosgrove wasn't that good at hiding what was in his soul. Everything in his conniving head was all right there in those eerily blue eyes hazed by the webbing smoke from his cigar.

"I got no damned idea, Kosgrove. Now, get the hell out of here!"

"You have a guilty look."

"Don't we all?"

Yakima took another pull from the bottle then got to work, climbing up out of his chair and scouring the cluttered shelves of the office for an old shirt—a relatively clean one. When he found what he was looking for, he tore the sleeves off the shirt, folded it up tightly, placed a whiskey-soaked poultice over the wound, then wrapped the bandage over it. He tied it tightly, knotting it over the bullet burn; it made a small bulge.

The exertion fatigued him, the whiskey-soaked poultice burning, biting him deep. He fell back into his chair and looked up to see Kosgrove grinning down at him, the mischievous light having returned to his malevolent little eyes.

"You still here?" Yakima growled.

"I was just enjoying your pain." The businessman puffed his cigar.

"Well, now that you've enjoyed it, you may take your leave."

"Your pain is just beginning, Henry. If you don't haul your freight out of my town, the pain will get much worse for you."

"I'll leave when I'm ready."

"Julia knows about you. You can't have her—not that you ever could have had her. Why not leave now...before I wire the U.S. Marshal's office in Prescott? Why let this get messy, Henry? I don't want to have to call in the marshals." Kosgrove threw out his hands. "Just leave. You can make this very simple for all of us!"

Anger burned up from the nasty grief in Yakima's left side. He hardened his jaws at the old man standing like an over-dressed walrus before his desk, slammed a fist onto the desk, and bellowed, "Get the hell out of my office before I blow your head off, Kosgrove!"

Kosgrove's eyes flared anew. He glanced toward the window, wondering if anyone had heard the tone in which one of his inferiors had addressed him. "You can't talk to me that way!"

Smiling, Yakima released the keeper thong from over the hammer of his stag-gripped .44. He slid the heavy piece from its holster thonged low on his right thigh, and aimed it out over the desk, slanting it upward as he drew a bead on the center of Kosgrove's forehead, just below the narrow brim of the man's bowler hat.

Kosgrove laughed. "Don't think I'm afraid of you, you half-breed bum!"

Fury coursed through every vein and artery in Yakima's large, husky body. It made his ears ring and his eyes throb. It didn't matter where you went, how far you climbed—if your skin owned a definite copper tint and your hair was as black as a Colorado mountain midnight, people would always see the Indian in you first. And last.

To them, you were no more than a dog. A half-wild dog, in Yakima's case. Even more frightening.

Staring into the big half-breed marshal's hard jade

eyes, Kosgrove must have realized his mistake. Wariness touched his own gaze a half-second before the Colt bucked and roared in Yakima's hand.

"*Ach!*" Kosgrove stumbled backward against the wall by the door, brushing his left hand across his ear. He looked at the hand and glared in astonishment at Yakima still holding the smoking Colt in his big, clenched, copper fist. "You did it! You shot me!"

He held out his little paw to display the blood on it.

Kosgrove brushed his ear once more. Again, his fist came away with blood from the little notch Yakima had drilled through the outside of the oversized appendage. A scarlet blood drop dribbled down that ear toward the lobe.

Yakima smiled savagely up at the man—through the smoke from Kosgrove's cigar as well as the powder smoke Yakima had added to the haze. "Get out."

The quiet mildness in his voice belied the savagery of his gaze.

Kosgrove wheeled quickly for such a cumbersome man, and, cursing under his breath, wheezing with anxiety and rage, he clambered out the door and down the porch steps. The thunder of quick boots replaced the harried taps and scrapes of the old man's shoes on the porch, and a second later Galveston Penny poked his head into the office, his eyes wide and white-ringed.

He held one of his own fancy new Colts in his right hand.

"Wha—?" the kid gasped. He glanced over his shoulder at Kosgrove still negotiating his clumsy way across the busy, dusty street. "What the hell?"

"Just took a notch out of that old ramrod's ear for him." Yakima grinned as he holstered the Colt. "Somethin' to remember this low-down, dirty, good-for-nothin' half-breed by."

Lower jaw hanging, Galveston turned his head to look toward Kosgrove once more. When he turned his head back to Yakima, the lawman said, "Run over to Hole 39 and fetch me a bottle of their cheapest rye." Yakima held the bottle he'd been drinking out of up to the window. "Ain't much left in this one."

"There's a whole two thirds of it left."

"That's not enough." Yakima flipped a silver dollar through the air. Lunging, Galveston caught the coin against his chest. "Run, boy!"

When the kid had hustled on out the door, Yakima sat back in his chair, sucking on the bottle. His mind was racing. He was angry and feeling sorry for himself by turns. He'd outstayed his welcome here in Apache Springs. He loved a woman but couldn't have her because of the color of his skin and the wildness of his ways.

Another home, gone. Another woman, lost.

He wasn't leaving because Hugh Kosgrove had ordered him out of town. He was leaving because Apache Springs had become a box canyon. He faced a rock wall. There was only one way out—the same way he'd come in.

He held up the bottle again, stared at the level of the whiskey.

First things first.

When Galveston returned with a fresh bottle, Yakima rose from his chair. He removed his cartridge belt and Colt and sheathed bowie knife from around his waist. He coiled the belt around the holstered Colt and the knife, and laid the works on the desk.

"What're you gonna do?"

"I'm gonna get drunk."

"Huh?"

Yakima picked up both bottles and walked into one of the jail cells running along the office's back wall. He set the bottles on the lone chair in the cell then drew the door closed with a heavy steel *bang!* He twisted the key in the lock, tossed the key to Galveston, and stared pointedly through the bars at the young man.

"You hold onto that until I'm back on my leash, understand?"

Galveston just stared at him, holding the heavy key and ring against his chest, lower jaw hanging, his eyes as wide and round as two full moons. "I don't...I don't..."

"I'm gonna get good an' drunk. You keep me in here, understand? No matter how I demand and threaten you to let me out, you keep me right here. Do I make myself clear?"

"No, no...I don't..."

"When I get drunk, I tend to get wild-crazy-mean. I've been known to destroy one saloon and go onto the next and the next until there's nothing left but smoke and cinders down a whole town block. I don't want to do that here. So, you keep me right here until I've got my wolf back on its leash." Yakima took a deep pull from the bottle, then another. Scrubbing his forearm across his mouth, he said, "Oh...and kid?"

"What?"

"Don't take it to heart."

"Don't...don't, uh...don't take what to heart, M-Marshal Henry?"

"Don't take to heart the things I'll say to you when my wolf is runnin' free and wild, all right? I won't mean any of it. Most of all, you keep a good hold of those keys and my gun and knife. Don't let 'em get closer to me than that desk."

Galveston looked and sounded miserable. "Yak... Marshal...Marshal Henry—I just don't understand."

"That's all right." Yakima sat down on the cot and picked up the bottle he'd already started on. "You don't have to understand anything except the importance of keeping that door locked and any and all weapons far away from me. At least, till tomorrow. I'll probably have a collar on my wild side by sunup."

Yakima raised the bottle. "Salute, kid!"

8

Emma Kosgrove, aka the Wildcat of the Sierra Estrada, dropped her tin coffee cup with a start.

It landed with a ping between her boots. She kicked dirt on her small fire then, grabbing her Winchester carbine from where it leaned against a rock beside her, threw herself backward off the rock she'd been sitting on.

She rolled onto her belly and rose to her knees, quietly pumping a cartridge into the rifle's action. Staying low, she stared off through the chaparral, in the direction from which she'd heard a mule bray. Her buckskin gave a startled whinny where it stood tied to a picket pin behind her.

She sucked a sharp breath through her teeth, cursing. At the same time, she spied movement in the bristling chaparral and rocks before her. Hooves thudded. Suddenly, the movement stopped, and a man's voice said, "You hear that, Pa?"

Another, older man's voice said, "I did, indeed."

Emma cursed again. Heart drumming against her breastbone, she heaved herself to her feet and strode quickly through the brush toward the trail that led down from the tableland and into the canyon she'd vowed she'd protect at all costs. As she closed in on the trail, she saw two wagons stopped on it, a beefy mule in the traces of the first one, two stouter, younger mules hitched to the second one. The first mule wore a battered sombrero with holes cut for its ears.

An old man wearing a shabby, dusty opera hat and a beefy young blond boy sat in the driver's box of the first wagon. Two young men manned the second wagon. Emma recognized one of the two as the scrawny string-bean named Rusty Tull. The other was Rusty's cousin, Cash Bundren—tall and lean and with brown hair under a palm-leaf sombrero so battered and sun-bleached that it might have been taken off the body of some old Mexican prospector who'd died in the desert long ago, his body devoured by hawks and coyotes.

The old man driving the first wagon was Collie Bundren, who leaned forward over his knees, the single, old mule's leather ribbons in his gloved hands. The stocky blond boy beside him was his son Dewey, Cash's younger brother. They were all staring cautiously toward the slender, buxom, flaxen-haired twenty-year-old woman striding toward them, aiming her brush-scarred Winchester carbine at them. The tails of Emma's black duster buffeted around her long, slender legs clad in wash-worn gray denim that clung to her fine body like a second skin.

Old Collie Bundren reached for the Sharps rifle leaning against the driver's seat between him and Dewey. Emma fired a round, blowing old Bundren's dusty black opera hat off his head, setting free the worm-like curls of his gray hair to glisten in the brassy light.

"Bad decision, old man!" Emma chided the man as she stepped onto the edge of the trail.

"Pa, it's that girl!" Dewey exclaimed, his expression an odd combination of fearful exasperation and a weird male delight at seeing the pretty, wild blonde whom he'd seen before in Yakima Henry's office in Apache Springs. Emma was not so unaware of her charms...nor so humble...that she did not realize that to these men she was probably the manifestation of an erotic apparition from a young man's restless dreams, appearing as she had out of nowhere in this dry, hot, colorless desert.

From an old man's restless dreams, also, she thought, glancing again at old Collie Bundren.

Emma had met the Bundrens when Collie and his two sons, Cash and Dewey, had come to Apache Springs to meet their nephews and cousins, Rusty and Chickasaw. Only, by the time the Bundrens had arrived in town,

Chickasaw was dead and young Rusty was locked up in one of Yakima's jail cells for his own protection. Emma had found Rusty in the desert, near the canyon. Chickasaw had lain dead nearby. It had appeared the older Tull brother had stabbed himself to death, ripping out his own innards in a mad frenzy to release some vile creature inside him—perhaps the rattlesnake he and Rusty had both eaten that night in a stew.

The sudden, horrific violence—not to mention the scene of the snake slithering out of his older brother's lifeless body—had left Rusty in shock and speechless, in a state of utter helplessness. Or nearly speechless, anyway. When Emma had found him, all the young, rusty-headed kid had been able to say was: "Snake...snake...snake..." Yakima had locked him up so he couldn't hurt himself.

Emma had learned that the two brothers, Rusty and Chickasaw, had discovered the old church in the mysterious canyon, and they'd begun looting some of the church's untold wealth in the form of gold and ancient Spanish bullion. Doing so, they'd become the victims of the curse of a long-dead Apache witch who'd vowed death and destruction to anyone who looted the gold from the church and the canyon, which Emma had privately dubbed *Arroyo de la Muerte*, the Canyon of Death.

Her old, now-dead friend, Jesus, had shared with her the canyon's story, for Jesus, whom Emma had found living in the canyon, had been one of several generations of ancient Apache slave descendants who'd given their lives to protect the secret of the Apache gold, living out their lives in that very canyon. Jesus was the last of his people. He'd died when a rattlesnake had slithered into his bed one night for warmth, and hadn't liked the company.

According to Jesus, the gold was considered sacred by the ancient Apaches, for it had been mined by the witch's own people—local Apaches enslaved by the vile Jesuit priests who'd come to this country several hundred years ago to plunder the desert for its rich gold deposits. When an earthquake had destroyed the mines and killed hordes of innocent Apache slaves, the witch had placed a curse on the gold.

And a curse on anyone who found that wealth and tried to gain by it—to prosper off the sweat and blood... off the *lives*...of the generations of enslaved and brutalized Apaches who'd mined it.

Emma had no doubt that Chickasaw had paid for looting the church with his life, and that the curse would spread and more and more would die if the church continued to be ransacked for its blood-stained, misery-besotted riches.

"Yeah, it's her from town!" said Cash Bundren in the second wagon. "What the hell you doin' out here, Missy? Put that gun down! You take a shot at my pa again, an' I'll—"

He stopped abruptly when Emma swung the rifle toward him, keeping her cheek pressed up against the Winchester's rear stock, narrowing one cool hazel eye as she aimed down the barrel, drawing a bead on his sun-burned forehead below the sombrero's brim. Cash Bundren wore no shirt, only suspenders holding greasy broadcloth trousers up on his skinny hips. He was as dark as a Mexican, and he had a thin, patchy beard and one half-crossed, crazy-looking eye. He was an ugly, rat-faced kid around Emma's age.

"Trash," Emma said, flaring a nostril as she continued drawing the bead on Cash's forehead. "Ugly, Southern, hillbilly trash. I oughta just kill all four of you right now!"

"*Bahh!*" Cash cried, lifting both hands and scrubbing his hat off his head as though by doing so he was removing the Winchester's sights. "Don't aim that long gun at me, by god, or I'll paddle your behind you little whore!"

"Whore is it?" Emma grinned icily.

The old man, Collie Bundren, must have seen Emma's index finger start to squeeze the carbine's trigger, for he raised both his arms, waving them broadly and yelling, "Hey-hey-hey! Eeezeee, now! Easy, Miss, uh...Miss... Miss Kosgrove, was it?"

Emma slid the rifle back to the elder Bundren, a horse-faced man with sun-burned, hollow cheeks carpeted in several days' worth of beard stubble the color of iron filings.

"It still is," Emma said.

"Easy, now, Miss Kosgrove. There's no reason to shoot anyone here. We're no threat to you."

Ignoring the man, Emma lowered the rifle slightly and turned her enraged eyes to Rusty Tull sitting in the second wagon's driver's seat, on the other side of Cash Bundren. Rusty gazed at Emma warily, skeptically, stretching his thick lips back from his large teeth in a grimace against the sun. He wore no hat, and his patched denims and linsey-woolsey tunic were virtual rags. He was like a human scarecrow sitting in the rickety looking second wagon. No doubt more than a little soft in the head, to boot.

"Looks like you must've got your memory back—eh, Rusty?" Emma said, her voice pitched with cold accusing.

Rusty's scowl deepened, carving deep lines across his high, dome-like forehead. "Who're you?"

"You don't remember?"

"No."

Cash cackled out a sleazy laugh, speaking to Rusty but keeping his oily eyes on Emma. On her shirt, primarily. "How can you forget *that*, cousin?"

"That will be enough of that kind of farm talk, Cash!" Collie Bundren reprimanded his oldest boy. "You mind the way you were raised and treat the fairer sex with the proper respect they deserve or I will beat the hide off your behind!" He switched his gaze back to Emma. "Now, then, Miss Kosgrove—how can we be of help to you today?"

"You can be of help to me...and to yourselves...by turning those contraptions around and riding the hell out of here. Forget what you know about that canyon." Emma canted her head to her left, indicating the arroyo dropping away below them. It didn't look like a canyon from here, but only a boulder-choked gorge or dry wash. That's why hardly anyone knew about the canyon and why no one ever found it by anything other than accident, as Emma had herself nearly three years ago now, meeting old Jesus, who'd dwelled in the canyon alone for years, only a year or so before he died.

That's likely how Rusty and his brother Chickasaw had discovered it, too, damn their blasted hides...

Now she realized that the reason she'd lost the Bundrens' and Rusty's trail was because, likely having seen how much treasure was in the church, they'd returned to town for the second wagon and the two stout mules.

"I don't understand," said Collie Bundren. "We are merely on a little exploratory expedition, following the geologic indications downslope toward what we hope are some promising looking quartz deposits. A river appears to have passed through here—years ago, of course—possibly washing good color into those rocks, an'—"

"Bullshit."

Bundren scowled, his hollow cheeks pinkening. "Say, now, that's no way for a lady to talk. Who raised you, child?"

"I was raised by wolves, some say. And you, Mister Bundren, are a bald-faced liar."

Bundren's eyes blazed. "Why, I oughtta climb down off this wagon, cut a switch, and tan your bare bottom!"

"Can I do it, Pa?" laughed Cash.

"Stay out of this, boy!" Bundren straightened up on his wagon seat, and puffed out his cheeks. "Where we come from, ladies don't talk like that."

Emma gave a caustic laugh. "I don't care how ladies talk where you come from, Bundren. You make one move in my direction, I'll blow you through the smoking gates." She stood holding the Winchester in one hand, the butt propped against her nicely curved hip. "And you take one more step down this trail and into that canyon yonder, I'll also blow you through the smoking gates and into the smoking butane rivers beyond!"

"What is wrong with her, Pa?" asked Dewey Bundren, staring at Emma in wide-eyed exasperation.

"Vile creature," said the old man, wrinkling a nostril distastefully at the girl. "Pure vile. Thinks she owns this desert, she does."

Emma turned to Rusty. "You don't remember me?"

Rusty wagged his head. "Purely I don't, Miss."

"You remember what happened to your brother?"

"I…" Rusty turned his befuddled gaze to his uncle sitting in the wagon ahead of him. "I guess it was sunstroke. Or maybe that snake we ate had a sickness."

"That what he told you?" Emma cut her eyes to the old man.

Rusty didn't seem to know what to say to that, so he said nothing. He just sat there beside Cash, staring at Emma as though he was trying to read something written in a foreign language.

She turned again to the old man. "You don't understand what you're messin' in here, Bundren. You got no idea."

"Yes, I do." Bundren smiled with satisfaction. "I take it you know as well as I do. You've seen it—haven't you, Miss Kosgrove?"

"I have."

"You have no claim on it, I take it. If you had, you'd have taken the treasure by now."

"My only claim on that treasure is to protect it. You see, Mister Bundren, that treasure is cursed. If you take gold out of that canyon, the curse will spread and infect us all. All of Apache Springs. Who knows? Maybe the entire territory. Hell, it might even take over the *whole damn world*! Just depends on how powerful the old witch was,

I reckon. Old Jesus said her spirit still lives here. She's likely watchin' us right now!"

They all just stared at Emma, blank-faced.

Cash Bundren turned to his father. "She's addle-pated, Pa."

"Likely the sun," said the elder Bundren. "Too many days and nights alone out in the desert. You've been tracking us for a while now—haven't you, Miss Kosgrove?"

"Several days. I lost your trail a day and a half ago, so I thought I'd camp out here on the lip of the canyon on the off-chance Rusty remembered the route back down to the church, and you came this way."

"And lo and behold he did." Collie Bundren smiled broadly. It appeared an odd expression for his horsey face to make. Not at all an attractive one. "Two days ago, Rusty woke up from a long night's slumber an' started talkin' so's we couldn't shut him up. He remembered the canyon, the church, but nothin' much after his brother died... God bless the young man's soul." He glanced at Rusty and added as though for comfort: "You can rest easy in the knowledge that Chickasaw is in a better place, nephew."

Rusty looked back at him dully and did not respond. He looked a little like he'd been on a bender and didn't have all his marbles back in their rightful pockets yet. He had remembered the old church in the canyon, though, damn his hide...

Collie Bundren turned to Emma. "What in the name of God are you planning to do with that rifle, girl?"

Emma stared back at him. She looked down at the rifle; she opened and closed her right gloved hand around the neck, her thumb caressing the cocked hammer.

Good question, she thought.

9

Gazing shrewdly at Emma, Collie Bundren fingered the steel-colored beard stubble on his chin.

He said, "Perhaps we can work something out, Miss Kosgrove. I mean, I've seen the church." A greedy smile twitched across his thin, chapped lips. "There's more than enough treasure. We can cut you in, let you have what we don't take. I figured we'd fill both wagons with what's easy enough to load and carry, and leave the rest. I mean, how much money can the four of us spend? There's millions and millions of dollars' worth of loot in there."

The old man was breaking out in a sweat just thinking and talking about the amount of wealth he'd seen in the church. His eyes glittered as though reflecting the unseen gold. His lids drew down and his pupils dilated. He looked like a man about to be overtaken by paroxysms.

"Two wagon-loads would do us all for the rest of our

lives," he continued. "All that I ask is you don't tell anyone else about the church until we're out of here, on the way to California to see about exchanging the loot for..."

He let his voice trail off when he saw Emma shaking her head and pursing her lips. She too was sweating. Not from the heat or from thoughts of untold wealth but from the images of utter devastation caroming through her mind.

"I can't let you do it, Bundren."

"You can't stop us, you silly fool!" scolded Cash.

"Yes, I can."

"No, she can't—can she, Pa?" Dewey asked Collie.

"I ask you again," Collie Bundren said slowly, mildly, shrewdly. "What are you going to do with that Winchester, Miss Kosgrove? Are you going to shoot all four of us? Are you going to kill us in cold blood?"

Dewey looked up at his father again and said in a hushed, fearful voice: "She won't—will she, Pa?"

For a few seconds, Emma considered it. That's what she should do. But when she imagined shooting Collie Bundren out of his wagon, and then the boy, Dewey, and then Cash and Rusty, as well, her knees stiffened up and her hands began to shake. Revulsion filled her belly like a quart of bad milk.

She couldn't do it. She couldn't kill this old man and these young men in cold blood. For the life of her, she couldn't do it though she could practically hear old Jesus calling down from Heaven to her: "Do it, Emma! Kill them! *Disparales*!"

Jesus had killed interlopers before. He'd seen it as his sacred duty. Emma saw it as hers, and she hated herself for being unable to do it.

"Get down out of those wagons," Emma ordered, putting some steel into her voice. "Down! Now!"

They all just stared at her.

"I mean it!" Emma lowered the Winchester's barrel and triggered a round into the ground between the two wagons. All three mules jerked with starts in their traces. One brayed and shifted around on its shod feet.

"Jesus Christ!" Cash Bundren cried. "I do believe she means it, Pa!"

"Down! All of you!" Emma bellowed. "Or the next bullet is goin' into hide!"

"All right, all right!" Collie Bundren said, holding up his hands, studying Emma now with more wariness than shrewdness. Glancing at his sons and nephew, he said, "Best do as she says, boys. She's a stubborn one— she purely is. Purty she may be, but she's got the fire of murder in *her* eyes!"

Cash cursed and wrapped his reins around his wagon's brake handle. He began to climb down from the driver's seat.

"You—Rusty an' Dewey," Emma shouted, aiming the rifle threateningly, her heart pounding now with the gravity of what she'd suddenly found herself doing, "you both climb down the near side where I can keep an eye on you. Any of you try anything, the old man gets it first."

She swung the carbine toward where Collie Bundren was climbing heavily down from his own wagon, over the wagon's left front wheel.

"*Ohh!*" he cried suddenly, turning around to face Emma and dropping to a knee in the dirt. He slapped both hands to his chest and hardened his jaws, his face turning red behind gray beard stubble.

"Pa!" Cash yelled, running toward the old man. "You all right, Pa?"

"What's wrong?" Emma said, scowling skeptically down at the old man.

"Pa!" Dewey scrambled down off the wagon's near side and crouched over the old man, beside his bare-chested older brother, Cash. Rusty hurried up from the second wagon to stand over his cousins, gazing down with concern at his Uncle Collie.

"Oh…" Collie Bundren shook his head. He was staring at the ground, keeping both hands pressed taut to his chest. Both arms were quivering as though he'd been struck by lightning.

"What the hell is going on?" Emma said, keeping the

carbine aimed at the elder Bundren's bare head. "What're you tryin' to pull, old man?"

Cash looked up at Emma, his eyes wide with concern. "It's his ticker. He's got a bad one and it appears you've worked Pa up with all your hysterics, and it's tightening up on him again!"

"Pa!" Dewey cried, placing a hand on the old man's shoulder. "Oh, Pa—please don't die!"

Emma grinned, shook her head. "Bullshit. Get up, old man, or I'll shoot you where you are. I didn't just tumble off the old buffalo wagon!"

"It's true!" Dewey cried. "Pa's got a weak heart!"

"Get away from him!" Emma ordered. "Get away from him now. *Git!*"

When the younger man had stepped back away from Bundren, who kept his head down so that Emma couldn't see his face, both fists clamped taut to his chest, Emma stepped cautiously forward. She kept her right index finger taut against the carbine's trigger. She'd shoot the man if he tried anything. She purely would, and give the devil the hindmost...

She stopped a few feet in front of the man and planted her boots a little more than shoulder width apart. "Lift your head, Bundren," Emma ordered, her voice drawn taut. "Let me see your face."

Dewey was sobbing as he stared down at the old man.

Cash and Rusty both stared down at Collie Bundren, their eyes round. Emma would be damned if they both didn't appear genuinely worried. Something told her she was being hornswoggled, though.

She just had a feeling...

"I said lift your head old man! I want to see your face!"

Bundren kept his head down. His left arm shook. He was breathing hard, making rumbling sounds through his fluttering lips.

"Lift your head, Bundren, or I will shoot you now!"

Slowly, Collie Bundren lifted his head. His chin came up slowly. His face was swollen and red. He had his eyes closed. When his face angled up toward Emma's, he snapped both eyes wide open. He stuck his tongue out in a bizarre clown mask of a face, and loosed a bellowing guffaw.

"*Got ya!*" he shouted.

Emma's heart leaped with a start. She jerked backward a half-step. Collie Bundren thrust his right arm out and sideways, cutting Emma's feet out from beneath her. She tripped the carbine's trigger. The bullet flew skyward as she plunged sideways and down, the rifle falling free of her hands.

She hit the ground hard, the wind punched from her lungs, her head smashing against a rock.

And then the world turned dark and quiet and very painful.

***

Emma lifted her head with a gasp.

She snapped her eyes open.

She blinked them, hoping to rid herself of the nightmare images that had assailed her sleep. But the faces of Collie Bundren and his two sons and Rusty Tull did not fade off into the fog of unconsciousness. She had not dreamed them. They were still with her, as they'd been before she'd lost consciousness. Only, now the four men sat before her, forming a ragged half-circle around a low fire over which a tin coffee pot gurgled and chugged.

All four were spooning beans into their mouths, the juices oozing out from between their lips to dribble down their chins as they chewed. She saw that they were in the canyon, near the church. Turning her head to her right, Emma saw the old stone chapel hunkered near the base of the canyon's eastern wall, partly concealed by rocks and boulders that had tumbled down the ridge during the earthquake that had killed the Apache slaves. Oddly, the boulders had avoided the church, as though God or some higher power had wanted to leave it as a shrine to those who'd died filling it with gold.

It was dusk, and the pale of the stone chapel and the creams, tans, and beiges of the fallen rocks glowed in the weakening light, as though they radiated a burning luminescence inside them. The canyon walls were nearly concealed in shadows relieved only here and there by the saffron, coppers, salmons, and pinks of the sun tumbling behind toothy black crags looming in the west.

The air was cool and growing colder. Emma only half-noticed. What she noticed overall was a painful hammering inside her head, just beneath the crown. Secondly, she noticed the men's eyes on her over here near the fire, where she was leaning back against one of several half-dead sycamores stippling this end of the canyon and rising like pale, crooked witches' fingers from the clutter of rock from the fallen cliff walls. Her hands were tied behind her back.

Her ankles were tied before her.

"You're awake," said Collie Bundren around a mouthful of beans. He sniffed, raised his spoon to her, pointing at her chest. "I do apologize for my boy. A wanton, lustful creature."

Emma followed the old man's gaze down to where her shirt had been ripped partway open, revealing a good bit of her cleavage above her thin, cotton chemise. Two bone buttons were gone, leaving only small bristling threads to mark where they'd been ripped away from her shirt. The top of her chemise was partly torn and pulled down to reveal half of one of her pale breasts.

Anger and humiliation flared in Emma as she turned to

where Dewey and Cash Bundren sat spooning beans into their mouths. The young brother, Dewey, was crouched over one knee, eating hungrily and loudly, sniffing and snorting with every bite. Dewey was grinning, snapping quick, furtive glances at Emma. Cash sat on a chunk of ancient driftwood beside Dewey, looking a little sheepish as he also plundered his tin bowl for the pinto beans.

His left eye was dark, the lower lid showing a swollen crescent beneath it.

"Don't worry," Collie Bundren said to Emma. "He paid for the way he pawed you. I'd ordered him to tie you and when I saw him...well...taking advantage like that...I hit him good with the butt of my pistol." The old man turned an angry look at Cash sitting to his right. "And he'll get worse than that if he ever tries it again!"

Cash wrinkled his nose. He kept his head down, like a scolded dog, but when he looked up from beneath his brows at Emma, a sickening seediness touched his gaze that lingered on her half-exposed breast. Emma wanted to draw her shirt closed but there was no way to do that—not with her hands tied behind her. The old man might have outwardly disapproved of Cash molesting her, but in the short time she'd been awake, she'd seen Collie's own squalid eyes straying to her torn shirt.

Dirty bastards.

Dusty was the only one not casting quick, ogling

glances at her. Keeping his eyes on his bean bowl, he seemed genuinely ashamed by how she'd been treated.

"Hungry?" Collie asked.

"No. My head hurts."

Collie gave a crooked grin. "Sorry about that."

"You're a fool Bundren. You're going to get yourself and your sons and Rusty killed. Maybe others, too."

Chewing, Bundren glanced at the coffee pot hanging from an iron tripod mounted over the fire. "At least have a cup of coffee. It'll make you feel better."

Emma glanced toward where both wagons were parked near the church, their tongues drooping before them. "Have you taken anything out of the church yet?"

"Nope," the old man said, dropping his spoon into his empty bowl then poking his thumb and index finger into his mouth. He plucked a bean skin from between his lips and flicked it into the fire. "Gonna wait till mornin'. By the time we got down here and tended the mules and set up camp, it was already gettin' dark. We have plenty of time. No use pushin' it." He turned his head toward the old church, and his eyes glowed as though the fire had been suddenly built up, which it hadn't. "That treasure has been here a long time. No one's found it, I 'spect, 'ceptin' you and your old buddy Jesus…an' them three carcasses laid out for the predators."

He turned to Emma and grinned knowingly.

"You saw?" she said.

"Sure, sure—we seen 'em. Your friend Jesus do that?"

Emma drew her mouth corners down and nodded. Not far away lay the remains of three dead men. They were only sun-bleached bones staked out on the canyon floor. On the rock wall near the bones, Jesus had scratched in both English and Spanish: TURN BACK OR DIE. *RETROCEDEN O MORIR.*

It was grim business, protecting the canyon and the old church. Hard steps needed to be taken. Jesus had had the courage to do what needed to be done. Obviously, Emma had no such courage. She hadn't been able to do what needed to be done. Collie Bundren's party was still alive to plunder the gold.

Bundren tossed his empty bowl to Dewey. "You're on cleanup duty, boy." He spat on the ground, rubbed the back of his hand across his mouth, and turned to Emma. "'The acts of the flesh are obvious: sexual immorality, impurity, and debauchery; *idolatry and sorcery*...I warn you"—he wagged an admonishing finger—"...that those who practice such things will not inherit the kingdom of God.'" He raised an admonishing brow. "That's from the Good Book—Galatians, to be exact."

"Yeah, well, you'd best tell that to the witch," Emma said, snidely.

Bundren gave a reproving chuff and wagged his head.

"You got a shot of whiskey?" Emma asked him. "My head hurts like a son of a bitch."

"Just as I do not utter farm talk, neither do I or my sons or nephew imbibe in spiritous beverages. It's the milk of the devil."

"Well, I could sure use a shot or two of the devil's milk about now," Emma sank back against the tree, stretching her lips back from her teeth against the pounding in her head. She lifted her head to look at Bundren. "What do you plan on doing with me?"

Pouring himself a fresh cup of coffee, the old man said, "I assure you, Miss Kosgrove, that as soon as our wagons are filled, I will set you free. I just want to make sure you don't try to disrupt my intentions again nor send anyone else out here to do so."

Cash laughed then covered it with a feigned cough.

Collie jerked a sharp look at the young man, who sat with a blanket draped across his bare shoulders. Cash looked away and whistled softly. Dewey had been gathering up the dirty utensils, but now he stopped and looked over at Emma. He stared at her darkly.

Collie fired a peeved look at his youngest and said, "I told you to clean dishes, boy! Not to stand gawking at the girl!" He lifted his long leg and rammed the heel of his boot against Dewey's backside, shoving the kid violently forward. Dewey gave a cry and, nearly falling, dropped a couple of bowls and some forks.

"S-sorry, Pa!" The boy gathered up the utensils then hurried off in the direction of a nearby spring.

Emma turned to Bundren who was now whistling nonchalantly as he poked at the fire with a stick.

Fear was a cold hand splayed across your back. "You're a fool, Bundren."

"So you said." The old man smiled mildly. "So you said..."

Emma wasn't sure how she managed it, but despite the misery in her head, and her fear, she fell asleep. She had no idea how long she'd been out when something closed over her mouth, drawing her head back and to one side, waking her instantly.

She tried to cry out, but the hand held her mouth closed, making the scream only a low moan. Her heart raced, and cold sweat instantly bathed her. She drew every muscle in her body taut, awaiting the slash of a knife blade across her throat.

The killing slash did not come.

Instead, she stared up at the silhouetted head of a man staring down at her. A pale face hovered over her, sheathed by stars twinkling in the clear, dark sky above it. Rusty Tull stretched his index finger across his lips.

Her heart still racing but beginning to slow a little, Emma gave a feeble nod. Removing his hand from over her mouth, Rusty glanced over to where his uncle and cousins were dark lumps in their bedrolls on the other side of the fire that had burned down to gray ashes from which a single tendril of gray smoke rose.

The camp was eerily bathed in the milky light of a nearly full moon. The moon was so bright it was painful to look at directly.

Emma took slow, deep, calming breaths as she stared up at Rusty Tull. She heard the snick of steel against leather—a knife being slipped from a sheath. She suppressed an instinctual, terrified gasp a half-second before she felt the welcome slash of the knife's blade against the ropes binding her wrists behind her back.

When those ropes were free, Rusty ducked down out of sight and behind Emma, who lay curled on her side, to go to work on the ropes binding her ankles. While he worked, having some trouble with the stout hemp, Emma glanced over at where the Bundrens laying slumbering. Collie's blankets rose and fell heavily as he breathed, lying back against a flour sack. He breathed raspily; every fourth or fifth breath was a ripping, rattling snore.

Emma tightened her jaws, afraid the old man's snores would awaken his sons.

She glanced down impatiently at where Rusty was sawing at the final coil of rope, using both hands and grunting as he worked. She was reaching for the handle, intending to finish the job herself, when the final strands of the rope broke away from the knife.

She kicked away the torn pieces and hurried to her feet, moving quietly, looking at Rusty curiously. What was he up to? Was he freeing her or did he have other intentions? If he wasn't freeing her, she sure as hell would free herself—by smashing a rock against the young man's head if necessary.

The boy canted his head toward where her horse and the mules were tied to a picket line roughly thirty yards away from the camp, down canyon from the church.

He was helping her get away!

As he moved off toward the picket line, Emma picked up her saddle and saddle blanket. She paused as she glanced around for her guns. She thought she saw her rifle leaning against the tree near which Collie slept. In the moon's opal light and thick shadows, she couldn't find her pistol. She could take a gun belonging to the Bundrens, but she didn't want to push her luck. If she lingered here, scurrying around for a gun, she was liable to get caught.

Holding the saddle by its horn, she hurried off toward where Rusty's slender shadow was approaching the horse and the mules. She stepped around him, moving toward her buckskin tied on the north end of the picket line. She hoped like hell none of the other animals, unfamiliar with her scent, brayed a warning to the sleeping Bundrens that something was amiss.

As Emma tossed a blanket over the buckskin's back, one of the mules gave a start. It lifted its head, about to bray. Rusty grabbed its head in both his hands and slid one hand down over its nose, squeezing its nostrils closed and muffling the stillborn cry.

He spoke softly to Emma. "Uncle Collie intends to kill you."

Emma's heart quickened at the notion. "I figured. Do you know why?"

"He said since he didn't file a claim on the church, there was a good chance the Yankee law might see plundering the gold out of it as a crime. Especially when an ex-Confederate done it. They might say it belongs to the Spanish church or some such, or the Yankee government, and they might even arrest us. Uncle Collie don't trust the Yankees, says they's all still carpetbaggers at heart."

Emma snorted as she tossed her saddle onto the buckskin's back and quickly cinched the latigo straps, tossing another quick glance toward where the Bundrens slept. Collie was still snoring. Not a peep out of Cash or Dewey.

Breathless with anxiety, Emma quickly slipped a bridle over the buckskin's ears. "When your uncle realizes you helped me, you'll have hell to pay. You'd best take a mule and ride with me back to Apache Springs."

"Nah. He'll take the whip to me, but I'm used to the

whip."

"Rusty, ride back to town with me," Emma pleaded with the boy, taking up the bridle reins and leading the horse back away from the mules. "I don't want you to get in trouble because of me."

"I'll be all right."

"In that case, I'm sorry."

"For what?"

"This." Emma laid a roundhouse right against the boy's left cheek. The punch made a sharp smacking sound.

Rusty grunted sharply and fell in a heap. He lay groaning.

Two of the mules leaped around on their heavy feet, braying crazily.

Emma bent over Rusty, whispering, "This way they'll think you only helped me out to tend nature, and I busted your jaw and escaped. But, again, I do apologize, Rusty. You're a true gentleman!"

Over in the direction of the camp, she heard the others stir.

"What—what was that?" Cash cried. There was the metallic rasp of a rifle being cocked. "Who's there? Who's there?"

Dewey's higher voice: "What's goin' on? *Injuns?*"

Collie stopped snoring. He yelled raspily, "What the *hell...?*"

Emma swung up onto the buckskin's back.

"*Hy-ahhhh!*" she bellowed loudly. "Hy-ahhh, Buck. Let's fog some moonlight!"

She steered the buckskin off across the canyon. It was a dangerous maneuver at night and at a full gallop, but the moonlight lit the way. Shadows grabbed at the horse's hooves, but Buck had been in the canyon enough times to remember most of the many obstacles.

"It's the girl!" Collie Bundren yelled behind her, his voice muffled by distance and the hammering of the buckskin's hooves. "Gallblastit, anyway! After her!"

A few seconds later, rifles cracked behind Emma. She glanced over her shoulder to see the menacing flashes of orange flames in the shadows below the big, pale moon. The rataplan of rifle fire continued, bullets screeching around Emma, hammering off rocks. She crouched low in the saddle, her skin crawling with the prospect of a bullet slamming into her or her horse.

Soon she was far enough down canyon that the bullets were no longer a threat. The firing dwindled to heavy silence. Emma pulled her head up but her heart continued racing for a long time, peril's cold sweat bathing her.

10

Yakima woke up with a groan.

He lifted his head from the cot and received a blow from a sledgehammer for his efforts. He lay back, pressing the heels of his hands against his temples. He opened his eyes. No one stood over him with a sledgehammer. The hammer was inside his alcohol-soaked brain.

"Oh, my," he heard himself grunt, pressing his hands harder against his head, trying to get the infernal pounding to stop without success. "Oh, my...oh, my, my, my..."

"The bear's a stirrin'." The voice had come from outside the cell he'd locked himself in. It had sounded farther away than that—from the top of a very deep well. One that he lay writhing in agony at the bottom of.

Yakima lowered his hands, lifted his head again—this time slowly.

"Yep, it's astirrin', all right."

The voice belonged to Yakima's senor deputy, the oldster who called himself the Rio Grande Kid, which is how he'd been known in his much younger days when, at least according to him, he'd run afoul of the law to some renown on both sides of the Texas border. Now he was old—somewhere in his sixties though where exactly in his sixties he kept a closely held secret, and he'd lost most of his hair and gained enough weight to resemble a small black bear pre-hibernation. He was currently kicked back in Yakima's chair, behind Yakima's desk, his mule-eared boots crossed on the desk's edge, a stone mug of coffee steaming in his thick hands.

He had one arm in a sling. That wrist was wrapped. His face was cut and bruised. There were three or four sets of stitches in its fleshy, sun-burned, freckled mass, which hadn't seen a razor in several days and owned the gray stubble to show for it.

Yakima blinked at the older man, whose real name was Johnny Day, and after hacking phlegm from his throat and spitting it into a nearby slop bucket, said, "You look as bad as I feel."

"I bet I feel a whole lot better." The Kid lifted the mug to his lips, blew ripples on the black surface, and sipped.

Galveston Penny chuckled. He sat in front of the desk, sitting sideways to it, facing Yakima. He was eating a burrito and drinking a glass of goat's milk as per his breakfast custom which he'd carried up here from his family's shotgun ranch in west Texas. His old Winchester carbine, which had also followed him from Texas, leaned against the right arm of his Windsor chair.

"What're you laughin' at?" Yakima growled at the boy.

Galveston snorted a sheepish laugh and hiked a shoulder. He looked away and took another big bite of his burrito and followed the bite with a slug of goat's milk. The Rio Grande Kid merely glowered at Yakima and shook his thick, battered head in obvious disapproval.

"What?" Yakima said through a groan. "You never had a few drinks?"

Again, Galveston chuckled.

Yakima dropped his feet to the floor and heaved himself into a sitting position at great cost to his head. The movement inspired the sledgehammer wielding sadist in his head to really go to work pummeling the Apache Springs' lawman's tender brain. Yakima sucked a sharp breath through gritted teeth, squeezing his eyes closed against the rabid onslaught.

"Oh," he said.

"A couple drinks, eh?" said the Rio Grande Kid.

Yakima was baffled. Why did his head hurt so bad? "What in the hell did I…"

He let the thought trail off as he opened his eyes and saw the broken glass fairly paving the floor of his cell.

He looked around, his expression growing more and more exasperated.

At least six—no, make that *eight*—whiskey bottles lay in bits and pieces all over the floor of the cell. As his brain absorbed the inexplicable mess, it began to register the pain in his hands. He held them up before him, and his lower jaw sagged when he saw his knuckles were badly scraped and bruised, several swollen and the color of gun bluing.

He swiped one of his battered hands across his forehead. It came away bloody. Somewhere during his obvious debauch, he'd cut himself.

Yakima looked at the mess around him again. "What the hell happened? I started out with only one bottle."

The Rio Grande Kid and Galveston Penny stared at him dubiously. They shared an equally dubious glance, then turned their heads back to face Yakima regarding them through the bars of his cell door. "You had two a night," the Kid said. "You got roarin' drunk each night and caterwauled so's I couldn't stable any prisoners in here. You'd have deafened 'em, scared the holy shit out of 'em."

Yakima stared at the man in disbelief. "Each night?"

"No," Galveston told the Kid. "*Last* night he went through one and a half bottles."

"I stand corrected," the Kid said, drolly.

"Holy Christ—how many nights was I in here?" Yakima asked, aghast.

The Kid kept his reproving gaze on Yakima. "Four."

"Four nights?"

"That's correct," Galveston said, smiling timidly.

"We ain't fetchin' you anymore licker," the Kid said. "You can threaten us all you want, but you've had all you're gonna get."

Yakima looked at the mess again, slowly shaking his head. Half-formed memories were starting to return. It was like waking up in a deep fog after being wounded in a fierce battle. "I'll be damned." He turned to Galveston and the old Kid. "What'd I do?"

"What's it look like?" the Kid said with a wry snort. "You turned your wolf loose. Soon as you poured that first bottle down your gullet, you turned into a raging griz. I never seen the like. I mean, I've seen men get drunk an' go wild before, but...shit in a bucket...I thought you was gonna bust that cell apart and then the whole adobe building."

Galveston said, "We fetched you more liquor to get you to pass out...so's you didn't kill yourself beatin' your head against the bars and walls of your cell."

"I did that?"

"Certain-sure." The Kid chuckled again and dragged a hand down his face. "You laughed till you cried and then you cried till you laughed."

"You called out names," Galveston added. "People's names."

"Women's names, mostly," the Kid said. "But there was also a man's name." He scowled at the floor, trying to remember."

"Thornton, I think it was," Galveston said.

"Thornton, that's it."

"Bill Thornton," Yakima said, mostly to himself.

"You were bawlin' out a gal's name—Faith." This from the Kid.

"Faith," Yakima said, his heart thudding. His wife, now dead. Killed by men sent by Bill Thornton.

"You were also callin' for..." Galveston let his voice trail off. He looked at the Kid. The Kid looked back at him; his eyes dark, hesitant.

"Who?" Yakima said, squeezing two cell bars in his hands—squeezing so tightly that his knuckles turned white.

Galveston's cheeks flushed. He looked down at the floor, absently massaging his left temple.

"Julia," the Kid said. "I don't recollect which name you called out more than the other. I know—maybe they was equal. You screamed Miss Kosgrove's name so loud one night that she herself came over to see what in hell was goin' on."

"When she seen how you was carryin' on," Galveston said, "staggerin' around like a bear with one foot in a trap and rammin' your head against the cell door, she herself broke into tears and ran out, bawlin'." The boy shook his head slowly, his eyes glassy with amazement as he regarded Yakima through the cell door bars. "I never seen the like."

"Yeah, that was a new one for me, too," the Kid said. "Me an' Galveston got so damn worried we called for the doc. Sutton came over an' said there wasn't nothin' he could do for you. He told us to just keep feedin' you whiskey till you passed out. Maybe you'd die, maybe you wouldn't. Well, you ain't dead yet though you look an awful lot like some three-day-old corpses I've seen." The old man pointed an angry, defiant finger. "Make no mistake—we ain't fetchin' you no more whiskey. You're done."

"Yeah, I'm done." Yakima drew a breath, noting only a trifle lessening of the throbbing agony in his head. "Let me out."

Galveston started to rise from his chair.

"Hold on," the Kid said, waving Galveston off and canting his head skeptically at Yakima. "You ain't tryin' to trick us, are ya?"

"Yeah," Galveston said. "You done that yesterday mornin', too."

Yakima was thoroughly befuddled. "I *did?*"

"Sure enough." The Kid gave a droll chuckle. "I could tell you was lyin', though. I refused to open the door, an' you went into a rage until you done passed out again. When you woke up again, you demanded more whiskey or you'd turn us both inside out, so Galveston hustled you up two more bottles."

"Jesus," Yakima said. He'd gone on benders before, leaving saloons in total destruction, so he supposed he shouldn't be all this surprised. "Well...I mean it this time. Let me out. I'm done. I won't turn either one of you inside out."

"You promise?" Galveston asked.

"I promise."

"On a stack of Bibles?" Galveston prodded, looking more than a little nervous.

Yakima sighed. "Yeah, yeah. On a stack of Bibles."

The Kid and Galveston shared another skeptical look. The Kid shoved the ring of keys across the desk. Galveston grabbed them, rose from his chair, and strode haltingly over to Yakima's cell. Keeping his eyes on the half-breed lawman's eyes, as though waiting for sign of a further attack, he poked the key into the lock. He turned the key slowly until the bolt slid back into the door, and the door sagged outward.

Galveston stepped back quickly, his eyes cautious,

one hand dropping over a handle of a pearl-gripped Colt holstered on his skinny waist.

Yakima brushed past him. He opened the office's front door and stepped out, wincing and narrowing his eyes against the onslaught of the mid-morning light. The light and the street sounds were like being assaulted by a rabid marching band.

He dropped down the gallery steps, fell to his knees, and plunged his head into the stock trough. He held it under until he was about to drown then pulled it out, whipped his hair around his head, groaning at the sledge-hammer's assault to his brain, then stumbled back up the porch steps. When he'd taken a big drink of water from the rain barrel, lowering the water level by nearly three inches, he hung the gourd dipper back over the barrel and shambled back into the jail office.

He ripped his town marshal's badge from his shirt and tossed it to the Kid, who caught it against his chest. Holding the badge in both hands, the Kid frowned curiously at Yakima. "What the hell…?"

"I'm resigning. You're the new law in Apache Springs."

The Kid looked at the badge. He looked at Galveston before sliding his disbelieving gaze to Yakima. "What's goin' on, Yak?"

"You heard me." Hair dripping, his shirt soaked, Yakima crossed to the desk. He opened a bottom drawer and pulled out his gun rig.

Galveston stared in shock at the Kid, who stared in shock at Yakima. The Kid heaved his burly bulk out of the chair, making the chair squawk, and said, "Yakima, dammit…you're just hungover. You ain't thinkin' right."

Gritting his teeth against the misery in his head, Yakima buckled his cartridge belt and sheathed bowie knife around his waist. "Oh, I'm hungover, all right. But I've never thought righter. I've let grass grow way too long under my boots. It's growin' up through my soles so that I can feel it tickling my feet."

Crouching, the Kid opened a desk drawer. He pulled out a bottle and slammed it atop the desk. He pulled the cork out of the bottle, slammed it onto the desk beside the bottle, and said, "Lord help me, but there you go. Have a little hair o' the dog that bit ya!"

"Nope." Yakima turned to the Kid, grinning. He placed a hand on the older man's thick shoulder. "Why so long-faced? You've just been promoted." He glanced at Galveston regarding him with his lower jaw sagging nearly to his chest. "You're the senior deputy now…seein' as how you're the *only* one." To the Kid, he said, "You'd better hire another man. See if the skinflints on the city council will spring for a second deputy. This town's too damn big for only one. I been meanin' to tell 'em so but I been busy of late," he added ironically, glancing once more at the mess he'd made of the cell.

"Yakima Henry, I ain't qualified to be no chief marshal," the Kid said, bald-assed fear in the old man's eyes. "I'm old an' slow."

"That's not what I saw out in the country a few days back. In fact, I followed a long bloody trail of dead Apaches up to you and those stage passengers whose lives you saved."

"That was...that was raw luck! The luck of the foolish!"

"No, it wasn't." Yakima's grin broadened. "Hell, you're the Rio Grande Kid."

He turned toward the open door, but the Kid rushed around the desk to step in front of him, holding up his hands, palms out. "No, I ain't the Rio Grande Kid. That's just me fumin' the place up with my blather. I mean...I was the Rio Grande Kid, an' sometimes I like to still see myself as the Kid. But in point of fact, the Rio Grande Kid's done hung up his shootin' irons years ago. *Years* ago, Yak! I'm...hell, I'm just Jimmy Day now." He poked his thumbs against his chest.

"Kid, you're a damn hero," Yakima told him. "It's time you started actin' like one. Now, pin that badge to your shirt and put some spring in your step."

The Kid looked distastefully down at the badge he'd left on the desk. He turned to Yakima again, frowning his disbelief. "Really?"

"Really."

The Kid scrubbed his hand across his chin, pondering the badge. "Well...I'll be damned..."

"Put it on." Yakima patted the old man's shoulder again then turned to Galveston Penny. He held out his hand. "Galveston, been nice knowin' ya."

Galveston scowled at him, eyes wide and miserable. "Really? Just like that...you're gonna...*pull out on us*, Marshal Henry?"

"Call me Yakima." He canted his head toward the Kid. "He's the law now. He's your boss. Mind 'im."

Grudgingly, Galveston shook Yakima's hand.

Yakima walked to the door, pulled his hat off a wall peg.

"Where you goin', Yakima?" Galveston asked in a voice hushed with sadness.

Yakima stepped into the doorway, filling it, and stared out into the blazing desert light. He thought about the question for a time, and said, "I got no idea. But, then, I've rarely ever had one. I usually let my horse choose."

He moved down the ramada steps and into the street, heading in the direction of the livery barn, where his black stallion, Wolf, was stabled. The thud of galloping hooves rose behind him, growing louder until he couldn't ignore them any longer. His heart fell when he saw the long, flaxen hair bouncing on Emma Kosgrove's slender shoulders clad in a dusty checked shirt.

"Yakima!" the girl cried, aiming the buckskin at him, drawing rein when she was ten feet away, the horse locking up its legs and skidding several feet, until its head was inches from Yakima's chest.

"Ah, hell." Yakima gave his head a quick, single wag. "I'm outta here, Emma. Whatever problem you got, the new marshal of Apache Springs is in yonder." He jerked his chin at the jailhouse then swung around and continued heading in the direction of the livery barn.

"It's Rusty Tull and the Bundrens," Emma cried. "They've found the church!"

Yakima stopped. His heart sank lower.

Glowering, he turned reluctantly, slowly back around to face the girl on the horse once more. "What?"

11

Emma leaped from the buckskin's back. As her own dust caught up to her, enshrouding both her and Yakima, she stared up at him, her hazel eyes cast with deep gravity. "They found the treasure. Rusty got his marbles...and his memory...back, and he showed his uncle and cousins the old church."

"Is that where you've been all this time? Out in that canyon?"

"Tryin' to track Rusty Tull and the Bundrens, that's right. And I tracked 'em, all right." Emma glanced around to make sure no one was listening in on their conversation. "Right to the church. Or close enough that I knew that's where they were headed."

Yakima shrugged. "Someone was bound to find it sooner or later. You can go home now, Emma. Ride out to your father's place at the Consquistador and have a hot bath. I'll maybe see you again someday."

Yakima turned again and started away.

Emma dropped her reins and ran forward. She grabbed Yakima's arm, stopping him. "What in the hell are you doing, Yakima? What's this about the 'new marshal of Apache Springs'."

"I don't have time to explain. I sunk a root too deep here already. I'm pullin' out. Have a good rest of your life, Emma." He meant it, and once again he started to head for the livery barn when Emma stopped him yet again, this time by stepping out in front of him and blocking his way.

"They knocked me on the head an' tied me up," she told Yakima. "They were fixing to kill me. Look—one of those ugly, rotten boys ripped my shirt."

"Well, I bet you taut him he grabbed the wrong tiger by the tail." Yakima chuckled. "Like I said, I'm haulin' my freight."

He tried to walk around her but she stepped in front of him again. She planted her gloved fists on her hips and glowered up at him, her pretty, heart-shaped face flushed with fury, hazel eyes glinting bayonets of unadulterated rage. "Seems to me you're always pushin' on, aren't you? Just when things get good an' tough, there goes Yakima Henry—saddling his horse and running away like a jackass with its tail on fire!"

She screamed that last so loudly that she startled several passing horses and riders, who uttered surprised exclamations and, drawing back on their mounts' reins, whipped their heads around to regard the pair—the big half-breed and the pretty blonde—in the middle of the town's main trace, along the edge of the newly laid railroad tracks.

Emma's fury literally rocked Yakima back on his heels.

"Seems to me, *Marshal Henry*," Emma continued, screaming the words while balling her fists at her sides and rising onto the balls of her feet, "you're nothin' but a low-down dirty coward! Oh, you can handle a few rowdy drunks well enough, but when things get too complicated for you, you wheel and run! To the next mountain! To the next desert! To the next town with a cheap whorehouse desperate enough to take in an unwashed, uncivilized savage like yourself! So, go on, then! Saddle your horse and ride the hell out of Apache Springs! We don't need a cowardly half-breed lawman here! What a town like Apache Springs needs is a strong, brave man who'll stay when the chips are down! Go! Go on, you low-down dirty Injun!"

She'd lunged forward and was punching his chest now, making him stumble backward, reaching for her flying wrists. "Go an' do what you do best and *run*!"

Emma sobbed and wheeled. She strode off down the side street to the north, taking long, stiff, taut-armed, angry strides. She scrubbed a hand across her cheeks and continued walking.

Yakima looked after her. "Where you goin'?"

She stopped and wheeled back toward him, her words as bitter and loud as before. "To fetch a fresh horse from the livery barn!"

"What do you think you're gonna do?"

"I'm gonna do what you'd do if you had half a spine. Someone's gotta do it, so I guess that person's me!"

She swung around again and marched off to the north.

Yakima watched her retreating figure for only a few seconds before he glanced around him. The street had fallen suddenly, bizarrely quiet. He realized now in the aftermath of Emma's onslaught that traffic had come to a standstill in both directions up the busy main drag. Horseback riders and wagons sat dead still along both sides of the iron rails. The only movement was the dust settling between the tall false facades.

Pedestrians had halted on the boardwalks to stare toward Yakima, squinting against the sun, some shading their eyes with their hands or with newspapers or parcels. Yakima glanced at Cleve Dundee's handsome establishment, the Busted Flush, on the corner ahead and on his left, and saw that the saloon's broad front veranda was filled with men and some young ladies of the working variety also standing frozen as they gazed in shock at the incredulous half-breed lawman. Beyond the cross street to the west of Dundee's place, a dozen or so doxies dressed in all colors of the rainbow stood silently regarding him from the second-story balcony of Senora Galvez's tony whorehouse.

Yakima's heart thudded when he saw Julia standing on the boardwalk fronting the brothel.

She must have heard the commotion from the Conquistador, just beyond Senora Galvez's. Now she stood, as did most of the others at the town's center, gazing curiously toward the big half-breed standing near the newly laid tracks, looking around him with what was no doubt an expression of deep bewilderment and no little embarrassment at having been dressed down so thoroughly by Hugh Kosgrove's youngest daughter.

Emma had made quite an impression not only on Yakima but on the whole damn town...

Yakima couldn't see from this distance what expression Julia wore. Yes, he could. He just didn't want to, because she appeared to be staring at him with pity, maybe a little disgust.

His thoughts returned to Emma and he crossed the damnable tracks that had ruined this once-quiet town and that were laid over fresh ties that reeked of coal oil in the hot sun. He strode down the side street to the Apache Springs Livery & Feed Barn, a new raw lumber building. Like most of the other buildings in the newly rebuilt town, it smelled sharply of pine resin. Gramps Dawson ran the place but he was nowhere in sight though as Yakima mounted the ramp and stepped through the large open doors, he wasn't looking for the old coot, only for Emma.

She'd already picked herself out a horse, a sleek mouse-brown gelding, and was leading him up toward the front of the barn from an open stall door behind her. She had an eye for good horse flesh. Yakima would give her that. The grullo was small and it had good legs and a nice barrel—likely a stalwart little pony that could cover a lot of ground fast.

"Forget it," he said, it being his turn to play the adversary, resting his fists on his hips as he faced her squarely.

"Go to hell," Emma said as she approached, holding the gelding's hackamore and lead rope.

Yakima cursed and kicked a horse apple against a stall partition. "I'll ride out and have a talk with Collie Bundren, goddammit."

Emma stopped a few feet in front of him, gazing up at him, a slightly lower grade of her earlier rage still in her eyes. She studied him skeptically for a moment then said, poutily, "You will?"

"Yes, I will."

"I'll ride with you."

"No." Yakima shook his head. "You stay here." He held up a commanding finger. "That's an order. A direct one."

She studied him for another second and then said in her pouty tone again, "Are you stayin'?"

"For now."

Emma dropped the grullo's rope and hurried up to him, closing her hands around his forearms, gazing up at him with hunger in her eyes. "Oh, Yakima. You know she's not for you. My sister's not for you." She reached up and slid a lock of his still damp hair back behind his left cheek, her eyes soft and passionate now. "You an' me—we're the ones who're meant to be together. We're both as wild as the desert!"

"Emma..." he started in a scolding tone.

Ignoring him, she continued with, "You don't belong in the Conquistador. Hell, a man like you don't belong in town. You belong out at that old adobe in the Javelina Bluffs—you an' me together. We can live out there, far from..."

Emma let her voice trail off as they both heard the approach of footsteps just outside the livery barn. Yakima's mouth turned dry when he saw Julia approach the barn's ramp. She was squinting against the sunlight, shading her eyes with her hand, trying to see into the barn's dense shadows.

"Yakima?" she called, tentative.

Yakima turned back to Emma. God forgive him for what he was about do. "Yeah," he said loudly enough to be heard outside the barn. "Yeah, maybe you're right, Emma. Maybe we should marry. It's you I love, after all!"

He drew the young woman to him, closed his mouth over hers.

He kissed Emma but his mind was on Julia. He could see the older Kosgrove daughter standing just outside the barn, at the bottom of the ramp, staring in from beneath a shielding hand. He heard her draw a sharp breath that was half a groan. She stumbled backward as though she'd been slapped. She wheeled and strode away.

When she was gone, Yakima pulled his head back from Emma's, released her from his brawny grip. She smiled up at him, intimately. "Yakima..."

Heart hammering his breastbone, he stepped back away from her. "Stay in town. I'll be back soon."

She considered that, pulling her mouth corners down, then nodded. "Okay. Be careful."

He barely heard that last admonishment beneath the clattering bells inside his head, aggravating his hangover. He retrieved his saddle and bridle from the tack room then, without glancing again at Emma, his mind on Julia striding away from him, heartbroken, he pushed through a side door into the corral to saddle his horse.

***

Yakima wasn't a mile out of town before he had to rein his big black stallion, Wolf, to a halt. He half-fell out of his saddle, hit the ground, and promptly aired his paunch. Since there was nothing in his belly, he vomited only bile.

The same thing happened two more times as he rode southwest of Apache Springs. He wasn't sure if his nausea was due to the hangover or for what he'd just done to Julia, ending their relationship once and for all, or to the overall mess he'd gotten himself into in Apache Springs.

Likely, it was everything, hangover included.

After the third time he'd had to vanquish his innards of the sickness eating away at them, he heaved himself uncertainly to his feet, uncapped the canteen he'd filled with cool well water before leaving town, and took several deep pulls. The water plunged down his throat and into his belly, instantly making him feel a little better and tamping down the heat that was raging from his own inner furnace.

When he'd capped the canteen and hung it over his saddle horn, he stepped back to his saddlebags. Emma had retrieved a ham and egg sandwich from the Bon Ton Café in Apache Springs. She run out into the street as Yakima had been leaving town and, trotting along beside him, she'd dropped it into his left saddlebag pouch.

"For when you bottom out," she told him. She'd recognized from his deathly pallor that he was in a bad, bad way.

At the time, Yakima hadn't been able to think about the food without that alone making him ill. Now, however, he'd needed something inside him.

He grabbed the sandwich wrapped in cheesecloth out of his saddlebag, mounted Wolf, and booted the horse on down the narrow trail through the chaparral. As he rode, he took large bites out of the sandwich. With each bite he felt the slow return of his strength and overall health despite the whiskey sweat still oozing from every pore.

"Thanks, Emma," he muttered, chewing the last bit of the sandwich and tossing the cheesecloth into the hot, dry wind. "You're not bad. No, not bad at all…"

Maybe she'd been right. Maybe he should throw in with the girl. They could hole up out in that old adobe in the Javelina Buttes, and…

He shook his head. That was just the sandwich and the hangover talking. And the warm, supple, female way she'd felt in his arms an hour ago, her pliant lips pressing against his own, her breasts swelling against his chest as he'd kissed her.

Again, he shook his head. It might be nice to think about—shacking up with a pretty girl like he'd once done with Faith. But Faith was the only woman he could have stuck it out with. She'd been special. There was only one Faith and she was moldering in a grave up in Colorado. If he tried hitching up with any other woman, they'd be at each other's throats within a month.

He had to get out of this country. Everything was closing in on him. Just as soon as he'd settled this matter with the Bundrens and Rusty Tull, he'd pull his picket pin. His home was the tall and uncut, the high and rocky, the distant mountains, the lonely canyons and arroyos.

He'd die out there someday, no one around to bury him. And that was just fine with Yakima Henry.

12

It took Yakima another hour to find his way down into
that lost, unnamed canyon—the canyon that had shown
up on no official map but only in the wild scribblings of
a sun-crazed pilgrim or two who'd stumbled on it by
accident and whose hearts had nearly exploded when
they'd spied the treasure there in the little, ancient church
built by the Jesuits. The chasm wasn't easy to find even
when you'd visited previously, for it was hidden behind
a jumble of rocks and boulders and bristling chaparral
stippling a slope rising gently toward the canyon's lip.

Finally, Yakima picked out horse and wagon tracks in
the chasm's general vicinity. The Bundrens' tracks, most
likely. He followed the sign through a narrow corridor
that penetrated the rubble and then down the long, gentle
slope toward the canyon's bottom. The sign indicated that
the two wagons had meandered through the rocks and

boulders and jutting cactus. Yakima saw where they'd stopped and where Emma had apparently confronted them. There were signs of a scuffle, and blood on a rock.

Emma's blood.

That made Yakima's heart quicken unexpectedly. He had no feelings for the girl. At least, he told himself he didn't. Still, seeing her blood there on that rock lit a fire of anger just behind his heart. He didn't like it that they'd hurt her. He didn't like that at all.

He'd dismounted to inspect the mix of prints. Now he took another deep pull from his canteen and poured some water over his head. Normally in the desert, he'd ration himself, but he'd find more water on the canyon floor, in a well by the old church. He mopped his sweaty, dusty face with his bandanna, set his hat back on his head, then swung back up onto Wolf's back. He urged the stallion on down the slope.

Fifteen minutes later, he reached the canyon's rubble-strewn floor and headed southwest along the base of the canyon wall. Not only was the canyon hard to find from up on the desert, but the church was hard to find even once you were down *inside* the canyon, for it looked like just another one of the cracked and half-pulverized boulders that lay strewn around it, some as large as the hovel itself, which was roughly the same size as your average house of worship in any frontier settlement.

Yakima drew up to the old place, its mottled tan walls cracked and pitted and streaked with white bird stains. One wall was crumbling, as was the belfry. A shadow leaned out from the church's right front corner as the sun angled high over the canyon, starting its westward descent. Yakima looked around carefully, spying no one. There were signs of recent visitors, including wagon and horse tracks, but at the moment the place looked deserted.

Deserted except for a Mojave Green rattler poking its head and several inches of its thick, stone-colored body out of the base of the church's cracked wall, on the lower right front corner, just right of the large, empty doorway. The snake stopped, apparently spying Yakima, probing the air with its dark, forked tongue. The viper formed a V as it began retreating back into the crack through which it had started.

"Hello the church!" Yakima called.

The only response was the tom-tom like beat of insects in the brush and rocks surrounding the place and the piping of desert birds. A wind had picked up and was making a low roar as it rolled up and down the canyon, lifting small curtains of swirling dust. It blew Yakima's long hair around his cheeks and shoulders.

"Hello!" he called, louder this time. "Collie Bundren, it's Yakima Henry from Apache Springs!"

Still, there was only the birds and the insects and the wind.

"Rusty!" he yelled.

He rode into the chaparral flanking the church, to old Jesus's personal quarters, which was a small, crumbling stone cabin. Nothing there, either. It didn't look like the Bundrens had discovered it, for there was no recent sign around the place, which was even better concealed than the church. Emma had introduced Yakima to Jesus's cabin not long after Yakima had first come to this godforsaken, trouble-bit country, soon after he'd met wild Emma out in the desert and she'd contested him for the deer they'd both been hunting but which Yakima had shot.

He rode back to the church, took a quick look inside, his heart catching at the sight of all the treasure there— the walls were literally paneled in old, age-begrimed, dusty gold, and more treasure was mounded atop the ancient altar, inside a moldering Spanish treasure box. The floor was even made of gold tiles! The Jesuits had parked a gold cannon inside the church, as well. All told, the treasure hidden away inside the ancient ruin must have reached into the many millions of dollars.

More money than Yakima would know what to do with. More money than he could do anything *good* with, that was for sure. He wanted no part of it. Besides, he was just superstitious enough to believe in a vague, half-conscious way in the hex Emma claimed the old Apache witch had put on the treasure and thus on anyone trying to abscond with it.

He turned Wolf around to face down canyon.

He couldn't see much. The canyon was long and bottle-neck shaped at this end, its floor choked with sand- and limestone debris that had plunged from the high ridge walls during the earthquake that had killed the Apache slaves. Brush and cacti of all shapes and sizes grew among the rubble, making it a devil's playground in which only the smaller and fleetest footed of the desert creatures forayed.

Peering to his left, he frowned. He saw something in that direction, maybe fifty yards away, that he hadn't seen before. He clucked Wolf toward the curious object, then reined up to stare down at the grisly images of what he'd seen before—three skeletons staked out on the ground beneath the warning Jesus had scratched into the lower ridge wall:

TURN BACK OR DIE. *RETROCEDEN O MORIR.*

The three skeletons now appeared to have some company. A large pile of rock fronted the three dead men. The pile was roughly oblong and maybe three feet high. The stones had been piled recently—within the past several hours, for the tracks around the pile were fresh. There were boot tracks as well as the tracks of shod horses.

Brown streaks marked the cactus and red caliche around the pile—dried blood, perhaps.

Yakima swung down with a sigh. The ride, in his less than peak condition, had worn him out. The heat and the sun and glaring light hadn't done his head a bit of good though he'd gotten rather good at suppressing pain. He'd endured a lot of it, so he knew it well.

He took another long pull off the canteen, making a mental note to be sure and refill the flask before leaving here. He didn't want to cap off his tumultuous stay in this country by dying of thirst in the desert, especially when he didn't need to. The well was over by Jesus's stone shack; he'd been too preoccupied with locating the Bundrens and Rusty Tull to have remembered to fill the flask earlier.

Also, his brain was still fogged by the whiskey. He'd have sworn off all tangleleg from here on in if he didn't know himself well enough by now to know that such a proclamation would be a load of goat shit...

He hung the canteen over his saddlehorn, shambled over to the rock pile, and removed one of the rocks. He let it roll to the ground, then unseated another and another. He'd doffed his hat and was working up an honest, working sweat when, removing yet another rock from the pile, he peered through the cracks in the rocks to see a brown eyeball staring back at him.

Yakima gave a sharp grunt and stumbled backward,

getting his spurs entangled with the ground and dropping to his butt. His heart hiccupped, and his quickening pulse aggravated that sledgehammer-wielding sadist in his head. His cheeks warmed with chagrin, he looked around quickly, automatically, making sure no one had seen his embarrassing display.

Reassured that he was alone out here—alone save for the owner of that brown eye glaring up at him through the rocks—he heaved himself back to his feet and moved tentatively toward the stones once again. He crouched over the pile, wincing down at the widely staring eye, and removed the rocks around it until he'd fully revealed the head and pasty face of Collie Bundren—complete with a quarter-sized bullet hole in the dead center of his forehead.

"Holy...shit..."

Yakima reached to remove another stone. Something screeched over his left shoulder and slammed into the wall of the cliff just beyond him. Wolf whickered and tossed his head. As the crash of the rifle rose from behind Yakima, he spun with a curse and, dropping to a knee, jerked his stag-gripped Colt from its holster. He sent three bullets hurling toward where smoke puffed between a long, oblong boulder and a one-armed saguaro.

A scream rose. There was the thud of a falling body accompanied by the clatter of a rifle.

Yakima rose and hurried forward. As he did, he heard someone gain their feet and begin running off through the rocks and chaparral. He pushed between the oblong boulder and the saguaro and caught a glimpse of a slender back and long, dancing, dark-red hair before the man darted behind another boulder.

"Stop or I'll shoot!"

Yakima broke into a run, spying an old Spencer repeater lying on the ground to his right. He weaved his way through the chaparral, following the ambusher's path. He ran between two more pale boulders. Ahead of him, the shooter was running in a shambling, heavy-footed way across a sandy arroyo, heading for a nest of rocks on the other side.

Yakima lengthened his strides and dove forward, knocking one of the shooter's booted feet out from beneath him. The man screamed again and hit the ground. Yakima was on top of him, grabbing a shoulder curtained by long, dusty hair, and brusquely turned the man onto his back.

Boy, rather...

"No! Stop!" cried Rusty Tull, staring fearfully up at Yakima, clutching his upper left arm with his right hand. Blood bubbled up between his fingers.

"Rusty!"

"Stop!" the boy cried. "Leave me be, damn you!"

Yakima glared down at him, his indignation at almost having his head blown off slow to fade. "Why in the hell did you shoot at me?"

As the boy continue to stare up at him, eyes glazed with both terror and befuddlement, Yakima realized that Rusty didn't recognize him. "You don't remember me."

Rusty just stared at him, stretching his lips back from his teeth in pain, squeezing his wounded arm. Obviously, he had no—or at least a foggy memory—of Yakima. In town, the boy had been addled. He'd still been addled when he'd left. His eyes no longer owned that addled glaze, but he seemed not to recognize the half-breed, who rose to his knees and then to his feet, slowly returning his hogleg to its holster on his right thigh.

He was tightening his jaws against the pain in his head which kicked up again when he'd made that dive.

Rusty frowned as he stared up at him, still breathing hard. "I have...a vague recollection..."

"We met in town. I'm...er, I was...the Apache Springs Marshal."

Still, Rusty only stared curiously up at him, trying to remember.

"Why'd you take that shot at me?"

"I thought...you was...one of them..."

"One of who?"

"You ain't?"

"No, I ain't. One of who—one of the men who killed your uncle, I take it?"

Tears glazed the boy's eyes, and he gave a single nod. He winced and glanced down at his wounded arm.

"I'll take a look at that." Yakima dropped to a knee beside Rusty. The boy jerked away from him, his fear quick to return. "Easy, boy. Easy. I'm a friend…of sorts."

"You are?"

"Reckon."

Yakima pried to boy's gloved right hand from his left arm, and inspected the wound.

"I think I do remember you," the boy said. "Big… Injun?"

Yakima gave a wry snort. "I'm right memorable. That doesn't look too bad. I'll pour some water on it and wrap it. It'll hold you till we get back to town." He looked at the kid resting back against the arroyo's low bank. "What happened out here? Your cousins dead, too?"

Rusty drew his mouth corners down and looked at the ground. "Yes. I buried all three of 'em in them rocks… after I worked my way back to the camp an' found 'em—all three—layin' dead."

"Who killed 'em?"

"I didn't get a good look at 'em. Uncle Collie—he was awful mad when that girl got away. He knew I turned her loose though I tried to lie an' tell him it was an accident. He started to skin my backside good with a quirt, an' I run away from him. He sent Cash after me but Cash turned and ran back to the camp when we heard horseback riders. I hunkered down in the rocks, and that's when I heard shoutin' and all sorts of harsh words, and then...the shots came. I heard Collie and Cash and Cousin Dewey all screamin'. An' then the screamin' stopped and so did the shootin'."

Tears dribbled down the boy's dusty cheeks, and his lips quivered with emotion.

"When I heard the riders leave, I made my way back to the camp." Rusty was sobbing now, tears dribbling onto the ground between his raised knees. "I found 'em...all three of 'em...dead." He sniffed, brushed his fist across his nose. "Everyone's dead now. Chickasaw's dead an' so is Uncle Collie an' Cousin Cash an' Cousin Dewey." He looked up through a golden veil of tears, sobbing. "I'm all alone now!"

Yakima remembered that Chickasaw was the boy's dead brother. It was Chickasaw's grisly death that had caused his mind to go soft, so that when Emma had discovered him and his dead brother and brought Rusty to town, the boy had kept muttering over and over again about a snake, as though he were in a trance and was seeing snakes all over the place. Then the Bundrens had come for him, and hauled him off into the desert where, apparently, he'd regained his senses along with his memory of where the treasure-filled church was.

And now his uncle and cousins were dead.

Maybe there really was something to that witch's curse, after all.

"Come on, kid," Yakima said, crouching to pull the boy up by his good arm. "Let's get you back to town."

Wolf gave a shrill warning whinny.

Instantly, Yakima's .44 was back in his right hand.

"Now what?" he whispered.

13

Again, Wolf whinnied.

Hooves thudded as the stallion ran off, the black's retreating rataplan replaced by the growing din of what sounded like two horses approaching at a hard gallop.

Yakima stood tensely, listening, his left hand still wrapped around the right arm of Rusty Tull, who stood quietly beside him though Yakima thought he could hear the frightened boy's heart drumming in his skinny chest.

The horses stopped about fifty feet beyond the arroyo, back near the makeshift grave. Men's low voices sounded briefly. One of the horses gave a rolling whicker. One of the two men said, "Tracks lead this way."

Yakima pulled Rusty back behind him. "Get down behind a rock."

The boy hurried into the chaparral and crouched behind a low boulder.

Yakima raised his Colt and clicked the hammer back softly. Slow footsteps sounded from ahead. There was also the soft chinging of two sets of spurs. The footsteps stopped and then Yakima heard the two men converse in soft, hushed tones.

Silence followed.

Yakima caressed his Colt's cocked hammer with his gloved right thumb, waiting, scanning the rocks and cactus before him, on the far side of the narrow wash. Following his boot prints, the men likely knew where he was—or his general vicinity, anyway. They should be along soon. Soon, Yakima would learn who else knew about the church, and who killed the Bundrens.

What a damn mess. And he wasn't even the damn town marshal anymore...

He kept running his gaze across the chaparral before him. He was sliding his inspection back to his left when he spied movement on his right, on the arroyo's far side. He switched his gaze quickly back to see a man stepping out from behind a saguaro and aiming a rifle at him. The rifle thundered, lapping smoke and orange flames.

The bullet snapped a branch from a creosote shrub just beyond Yakima, to his left.

Yakima dropped to a crouch, seeing in the corner of his left eye another man step out of the chaparral and into the arroyo, cocking a rifle. Yakima threw himself forward, hitting the arroyo on his belly, rolling right and barely avoiding another bullet before firing first at the first man who'd shot, and then, rolling in the opposite direction, at the man on his left.

The Colt bucked and roared twice before Yakima rolled back to his left and flung another round toward the first man who'd fired, on his right.

His bullet cut the air where the man had been standing, finding now only the implacable face of a boulder. The ricochet gave an angry, snarling wail. The shooter himself was gone.

Rising quickly to a knee, Yakima clicked the Colt's hammer back and aimed at the second man, on his left. He held fire. The man was down on his back, the bottoms of his boot soles facing Yakima. One leg was shaking. The man's arms were spread wide and he was digging his fingers into the sand and gravel, as though literally trying to cling to life.

He didn't manage it. His leg stopped quivering and then the rest of his body fell slack, as well.

One down...

"Stay where you are, Rusty!" Yakima yelled as he ran into the chaparral on the other side of the arroyo.

Running footsteps sounded ahead of him, retreating.

"Hold on, you yellow devil!"

Yakima ran ahead, weaving through the desert scrub.

A gun barked ahead of him. He only saw the flash, heard the bullet ricochet over his left shoulder. He threw himself right and rolled, and two more shots rocketed around the canyon.

Rolling up onto his chest, Yakima extended the Colt and fired two quick rounds. He tried to fire another one, but his hammer clicked benignly onto an empty chamber.

Staying down, half-expecting the man to come back for him, Yakima clicked open the Colt's loading gate, and shook out the spent shells. When he'd replaced two with fresh bullets from his shell belt, a horse whickered ahead. A girl shouted, "Stop!"

A man returned with: "Stop this, little gal!" A rifle barked twice.

The girl screamed and a horse whinnied shrilly.

Yakima's heart raced dreadfully as he filled the Colt's last four chambers, clicked the loading gate home, and scrambled to his feet.

"Emma!" he bellowed as he ran in the direction of the Bundrens' grave and from where he heard another horse whinny and then thud off at a fast gallop.

He ran out of the chaparral to see Emma on the ground near the Bundrens' barrow. She was sitting up, resting her elbows on her knees, pressing her fingers to her temples. Her long hair, dusty and tangled, hung down over her face.

"Oh, for chrissakes!" Yakima ran toward her. "You all

right? You hit?"

She looked up at him, wincing. "No. He didn't hit me. Thanks to my horse bucking me off." She glanced sourly over at where the buckskin stood a way to the north, its saddle hanging down its side, its eyes glinting edgily. Emma stretched a hand back behind her, massaging her lower back. "Just bruised is all."

"What the hell are you doing out here?" Yakima said, fetching her hat and angrily tossing it down at her. "I told you to stay in town."

She gave her head a wild-mare sort of toss and glared up at him, jaws hard. "You know I couldn't do that!"

"Yeah, well you almost got yourself killed for not minding my orders!"

"You got no authority to order me around, Yakima Henry. You quit—remember? The Rio Grande Kid is Marshal of Apache Springs now!"

Ignoring her, he stared off in the direction the bushwhacker had disappeared. "Who was that? Did you get a look at him?"

"Not a good one." Emma spat grit from her lips then scrubbed her shirtsleeve across her mouth and spat again. "They were followin' you. They got onto your trail about halfway out from town. I'm thinkin' they were headin' *toward* you and then got *around* you and followed you back to the canyon."

"I reckon they weren't the only ones followin' me."

"I saw what they were up to, an' I rode down here to warn you, you ungrateful half-breed son of a bitch!" She fairly screamed the tirade, her eyes glassy and white-ringed. She spat again then said, "Did you find the…" Just then she saw the all-but-exposed head of Collie Bundren poking up from the stone cairn.

Emma stared at the piled rocks, her mouth open. "Oh…"

"Yeah."

"What about—?"

"Cash an' Dewey are in there, too."

"What about—?"

"Here."

Rusty stepped out of the chaparral. He looked pale and world-weary, more than a little frightened. He was a sensitive boy, and he'd seen a lot of killing lately. The Bundrens may not have been much of a family to him, but they'd been all he'd had left after Chickasaw had died so bizarrely, stabbing out his own guts. Now he had no one. He was alone and he knew it and was feeling the raw cold lonely truth of what alone was.

He'd get used to it. Yakima had faced the world alone when he was even younger than Rusty. The boy would get used to it, too. As much as anyone ever could, anyway.

Emma got up and dusted herself off. "What happened, Rusty? Are you all right?" She was looking at his left arm, which he'd wrapped a red handkerchief around.

"I did that," Yakima said.

"It's all right," Rusty said. "I had it comin'."

Emma turned her head to the grave again. "Who killed...?"

"Whoever those bushwhackers are," Yakima said, then quickly amended the statement with, "Or *were*..."

"Where's the other one?"

"This way."

Yakima turned and headed back into the chaparral. In a couple of minutes, he, Emma, and Rusty were staring down at the bushwhacker whose wick Yakima had trimmed. He was a large, beefy, ginger-bearded man in a brown coat, white shirt, string tie, and corduroy trousers. His boots looked new. Flies had found the bloody hole in his chest that Yakima had drilled with a .44-caliber bullet.

The bullet had clipped off the very end of the man's string tie.

"Jack Booth." Emma looked at Yakima. "Shit!"

"What?"

"He rides for my father. He's a bullion guard."

Yakima knew that Hugh Kosgrove's so-called bullion guards didn't only guard Kosgrove's bullion. They were often trouble-shooters with the emphasis on "shooters." They took care of any and all problems their boss was confronted with. Being a man of considerable wealth and power not to mention a scorpion's personality, Kosgrove was understandably confronted with a lot of trouble.

Emma gave the nearest rock a furious kick. "That means my father knows about the church!"

"Well, that figures. It's not far from his land. It goes to reason one of his geologists would have stumbled on this canyon...and the church...eventually. Why he hasn't done anything with the treasure yet is right puzzling."

"Knowing him he's probably covering all his tracks—having his lawyers do whatever it takes to plunder treasure from an ancient Jesuit church. Leastways, so it looks legal, even if it isn't."

"I have a feeling that treasure is there for anyone who stakes a claim on it. That's probably what you should have done. Claimed it."

"God, no! I don't want any claim on that gold. By claimin' that gold, I'd be claimin' the curse, too! Yakima, you just don't understand!"

"Well, there's one thing I understand." Yakima was staring down at the dead man—Jack Booth. "Your father's men killed the Bundrens in cold blood. Likely would have killed Rusty, too. And they tried to kill me." He narrowed an eye as he stared pointedly at Emma. "There ain't nothin' legal about that."

"Okay, maybe I was wrong about the legal business. Why he's been waiting around to loot the treasure, I got no idea. But I aim to ask." Emma swung around and started walking back through the chaparral. "And I aim to head on back to Apache Springs and do just that!"

Yakima sighed as he stared down at the dead man. "I've a mind to leave this son of an ambushin' buck to the raptors." He rubbed his jaw, thoughtful. "On the other hand, it would be fun to see the look on Hugh Kosgrove's face when I tossed one of his men to him—dead. One of the men who killed the Bundrens and tried to do the same to us."

He glanced at Rusty staring gloomily down at Jack Booth. "Come on, boy. Let's round up this fella's hoss. We'll come back for Booth, then get to town. We'd best have Doc Sutton check out your arm."

"Mister Henry?" Rusty asked as he followed the former town marshal of Apache Springs back toward the Bundrens' grave.

"Yakima."

"All right...Yakima?"

"What is it?"

"What's Miss Emma mean about a 'curse'?"

"Oh, hell." Yakima gave another weary sigh. "Why don't you ask her? She's just crazy enough to make it sound convincing."

He gave a dry chuckle then, stepping out of the chaparral, whistled for his horse.

155

14

Trailing the dead Jack Booth tied belly down over Booth's own horse, Yakima put Wolf up the last stretch of sloping ridge and onto the lip of the canyon.

Emma and Rusty Tull came up behind him, riding double on Emma's buckskin.

Yakima halted his two horses to rest them after the hard climb in the early fall heat, and Emma stopped her buckskin beside him. There was more wind up here than down below. Beneath the soughing of the wind was a low rumbling roar, like that of a distant train.

"What's that?" Rusty asked, the boy's long, rust-colored hair blowing back from his face in the warm, dust-laden breeze.

Yakima felt a pinch of anxiousness and a nettling frustration. He pointed a gloved finger toward what appeared a dark wall in the northeastern sky—or a heavy, charcoal-colored curtain edged with an eerie, pulsating rose and lemon yellow. "That's what that is," he said.

"Huh?" said Rusty.

"Sand storm!" Emma said.

Yakima whipped a hard look at her. "Javelina Bluffs!"

He poked spurs against Wolf's flanks, and the horse lunged into a gallop. Yakima jerked Booth's claybank gelding along behind him and glanced over his shoulder to see Emma leaning forward as her own buckskin broke into a dead run, as well, the girl casting quick, frequent glances toward the wall of wind and sand approaching fast from the northeast.

A sandstorm was nothing to get caught in. Some could be deadly. Men and horses had been known to get so sandblasted that they'd suffocated, their bodies found poking out of fresh dunes, sand-basted feasts for swirling buzzards.

As the wall of sand grew closer, the train-like rumbling growing louder and louder, Yakima rode Wolf around a jutting finger of broken rock and turned him straight west toward the low bare ridges of the Javelina Bluffs rising straight ahead. He'd lived out there for several months when he'd first come to this country, having won a gold claim in a poker game and having nowhere else to go after killing the deputy U.S. marshal in a little town up in Kansas—a man who'd needed killing, by the way.

Several months hadn't been long enough to know this vast and varied country so intimately that he never got turned around in it. It happened again now, when he was confronted by two arroyos curving ahead of him, each bending off in opposite directions.

He slowed Wolf, frowning, trying to remember which course would take him to his old cabin. Emma galloped past him. "This way!" she yelled, and bounded off down the arroyo on the left and which hugged the base of a haystack butte as pale as alkali and capped with several rocks resembling horses' teeth.

Yakima grumbled with fleeting chagrin. But, then, Emma had grown up out here—as wild as a diamondback. Yakima whipped Wolf after the young woman and the rusty-headed boy.

Ten minutes later they leaped up and over the arroyo's left bank, and the brush-roofed adobe shack lay before them in a flat clearing ringed with rock-strewn hogback buttes. A stable constructed of ironwood uprights and a corral of woven ocotillo branches lay to the left of the shack. A well fronted the hovel, ringed with mortared stone and roofed with ironwood planks and brush.

The storm reached the shack's yard just as Yakima reined Wolf to a skidding stop outside the stable. Leaping out of the saddle, he opened the rickety door, which was missing a few slats in the bottom, and jerked with a start when a gray creature about shin-high bounced off his right leg and dashed off into the brush behind the stable. The creature had stolen a quick, frightened glance up at Yakima through its small, liquid-amber eyes, before taking its hasty leave.

Desert fox.

The harmless critter had kicked Yakima's ticker into fast motion.

He threw the stable's single door wide and waved Emma and Rusty in ahead of him. The storm was howling like seven witches out of hell, basting the old shack and stable with sand that bit like blackflies. Yakima held his hat on his head with one hand as he followed the other two and the buckskin into the stable, pulling his own and the dead man's horse in behind him. He shut and latched stable door, then doffed his hat and shook sand from his hair.

So did Rusty, looking up at Yakima with red-rimmed eyes. "This sorta thing happen often out here?"

Emma was already stripping tack from her buckskin's back. "I been caught in a desert duster more times than I can count."

"You oughta stay home more," Yakima told her with a grunt, unbuckling Wolf's latigo strap, then pulling the blanket and saddle off the stallion's back.

Emma whipped a glare at him, eyes flashing in the

stable's dense shadows. "And dress up in white linen and taffeta, tie ribbons in my hair, an' sit in front of the parlor piano, playin' Mister Chopin for Father?"

Yakima grabbed a swatch of burlap and began rubbing Wolf down. "Took the words right out of my mouth."

"You can kiss my—"

He returned her glare with an admonishing one of his own. "Not in front of the boy!"

Rusty gave Yakima a rare grin.

***

When they'd tended the horses, giving each a few inches of water from their canteens and a bait of oats, and Yakima had lain Jack Booth out against the stable's back wall, he closed and latched the stable door and led Emma and Rusty to the shack, one wall of which was bowed precariously inward.

The wind howled and moaned, sounding like a cheap whorehouse on a hopping Friday night on the border. The sand blew in dun waves, some waves denser than others. The sky was a washed out dark yellow color tinged with a sickly greenish red. The brush atop the cabin was bent nearly flat against the mesquite poles of the roof.

Yakima was glad to find that the only tenant that had taken up residence in and around the humble little earthen-floored shack was the fox. He'd closed the hovel up tight when he'd last left it, and it was still tight. A little too tight.

He'd placed a coffee tin weighed down with a heavy rock over the stovepipe. So now he endured the wind-blown sand to climb up and remove it. Holding a blanket over his head and shoulders, he also braved the storm to fetch water from the well.

When he'd built a fire and put the sulky Emma to work making coffee, he cleaned the bullet burn he'd given Rusty, and wrapped the boy's arm with a whiskey-soaked sleeve of an old shirt he found hanging from one of the many wall hooks in the shack, which he'd assumed had been built well over a hundred years prior and been lived in by one desert rat prospector after another.

He'd been the last resident.

"There ya are," Yakima said, knotting the bandage taut around Rusty's shoulder. "Might hurt for a bit, but you'll be good as new in a day or two."

"Thanks."

"Don't thank me. I'm the one that shot ya."

"I almost shot you," Rusty reminded him from where he sat the shack's single, small eating table, on a rickety chair minus its back.

"Oh, that's right." Yakima gave the kid a warm smile. "Don't worry—I don't hold grudges. If I want revenge on a fella, I do it right away or sic Emma on him." He winked.

Rusty gave a wan smile of his own then turned to gaze through a crack in a stout shutter closed over the window across the table from him. Yakima knew what he was thinking about. His uncle and cousins, all three of whom he'd buried under rocks.

"Don't worry," Yakima told the kid, laying a big hand on the back of Rusty's neck and giving it an affectionate squeeze. "They're in a better place."

Emma gave a wry chuff where she sat at the opposite end of the table from Yakima, blowing on the coffee she'd just poured. She'd poured one each for Yakima and Rusty, as well. The steam rose in the shack's shadows, limned with the weird yellow light angling through cracks in the shutters. The air was richly flavored with the bracing aroma of the fresh Arbuckles.

Emma fixed Yakima with a caustic sneer and said, "That's real helpful—what you told him. You must've studied to be a preacher."

"Yeah, well, that's all I got."

Emma sipped her coffee, swallowed, and slid her own sullen gaze to the young man. "It'll be all right, Rusty. You're better off without those three scurvy devils."

It was Yakima's turn to snort. "That's much better. Fresh from the nunnery, are you?"

"I'm all alone now," Rusty said. "Chickasaw...Uncle

Collie...Cash an' Dewey—they was all I had in the world."

"Yeah, well...like I said," Emma said as she lifted her hot tin cup to her lips with both gloved hands, and took another sip.

Yakima sipped his own coffee and turned to the young man. "You'll get by, Rusty. I'll see to it. I'll get you set up with a job in Apache Springs, and in no time, you'll be on your feet and fittin' right in. Hell, Apache Springs is a boomin' place. You'll soon have a stake of your own and probably even start wearin' a three-piece business suit."

He glowered as he blew on his coffee and added wryly, "Though I don't intend to stick around to see it. There's already too many three-piece suits in Apache Springs for my taste."

"You can say that again." Emma looked at Yakima. As though to remind him of what they'd learned before the storm hit, she said, "Pa knows about the church. The canyon."

"Looks like."

"What're you gonna do about it?"

"I don't know." Yakima looked at her sharply and with no little irony. "You want me to kill him?"

"Of course not. The old bastard's my pa."

Rusty glanced at her skeptically.

Understanding the dilemma, Emma pulled her mouth corners down and stared at the scarred surface of the old cottonwood table. "Somethin's gotta be done, though. If anymore treasure is taken out of that canyon..."

She let her voice trail off.

Rusty frowned curiously at her. "What'll happen, Miss Emma?"

Emma told him about old Jesus and the curse. The story held the boy rapt, eyes as wide and round as silver dollars though the color of copper pennies.

"So...that's what happened to Chickasaw? That snake came crawlin' out of him on account we took the treasure from the church?"

"That's right."

"Maybe," Yakima stepped in. The story had sounded all the more absurd for the truncated way Emma had explained it to the boy.

"Sure as hell!" she fairly yelled across the table at Yakima, causing Rusty to jerk so far back in his backless chair that he nearly fell off of it and had to throw his arms out for balance, spilling some of his coffee.

"Whoa!" he said.

"It's a fable, Emma. A tall tale. Old Jesus just wanted to protect that church, keep it from bein' looted. So, he told you that story."

"You're sayin' he lied to me?"

Yakima hiked a shoulder and sipped his coffee.

Emma smiled shrewdly. "You don't believe that."

"Yes, I do."

"Nope."

Yakima took another sip of his coffee.

"You know how I know you do?" she asked.

He swallowed his coffee and stared across the table at her.

"You haven't taken a thing out of that church."

"I have no use for trinkets."

"Everyone has use for 'trinkets'. At least one, maybe two. You could have dropped one of the trinkets from atop the altar into your saddlebags and ridden off with a nice stake for yourself."

Yakima felt a little warmth rise in his face. Maybe she was right. Maybe he was afraid of the curse. Still, he didn't want to think so. He didn't want to believe in it. He didn't like thinking that there might be even more hoodoo at work here on earth than the hoodoo of good old-fashioned men and women. That was enough hoodoo for him.

Emma and Rusty stared at him.

He turned away in annoyance and poked another log into the wood stove. "Why don't you make yourself useful, girl, and make supper?" He closed the stove door and crouched to peer through the cracks in a window shutter. The storm was still thrashing this hollow in the bluffs. "Looks like we're gonna be here awhile."

Emma cursed as she rose from her chair, scowling at him. "If it'll make you feel better."

Yakima dug his makings out of his shirt pocket and set to work rolling a smoke. He thought it might quiet his mind a little. But it didn't. All the different strands of the mess he'd gotten himself into here in Apache Springs kept entangling themselves. He wondered if he'd ever get himself entangled and be able to ride out of this crazy country in one piece.

15

Emma wasn't much of a cook, but she found a couple of airtight tins, one of beans, the other of beef, and heated the grub together in a cast-iron skillet. They made a satisfactory meal for the humble circumstances. The food took the edge off Yakima's hunger though he saw that neither Emma nor Rusty did much but fork the vittles around on their tin plates.

Their minds were elsewhere.

Not long after Yakima had finished eating, the wind died. The storm rumbled itself out like a train running out of steam on a steep upgrade.

Suddenly, the moaning stopped, as did the ticking of the sand against the adobe walls and shutters. Yakima stepped out onto the rickety stoop to a clear sky down the western horizon of which the sun was plummeting. Shadows grew long and dark.

It was too late to ride back to Apache Springs, so after the sun had gone down, and Yakima had scrubbed the plates and pan at the well, and he and Emma and Rusty had spent a quiet hour sitting on the stoop, watching the bayonets of sunlight in the west change colors then fade, he tramped behind the shack to evacuate his bladder then slouched off to the stable for some shuteye. There were only two cots in the cabin. He'd leave them to the younkers. He felt like being alone, anyway. He wanted to be nowhere near Emma after dark.

"There's a dead man out there!" Emma called to him as he approached the stable door.

"I ain't afraid of dead men," Yakima said, his quiet voice carrying clearly in the post-storm silence. There wasn't so much as a whisper of a breeze. "It's the livin' ones that give me the fantods."

"I'll come out an' tell you a bedtime story," Emma called again.

He pulled a stable door open and glanced back at her. She smiled crookedly at him from where she sat on the stoop, one boot hiked on her other knee. Hands entwined behind her head, she leaned back in her chair, letting her shirt stretch taut across her breasts. She gave him a lusty wink.

"No chance," he said, and pulled the stable door closed.

There was only one window in the stable, on the east

side, opposite where the sun was setting, so he stumbled around in the shadows before he found the old railroad lantern hanging from a wire looped over a moldering wooden ceiling beam. While he did, he heard a shuddering sound from the stable's west side. The horses were whickering quietly with subdued concern, so the sound concerned him, as well.

He lit the lamp, closed the soot-stained mantle, and held it high, tilting its light across the hay-flecked earthen floor toward the western adobe wall, which was badly cracked in places. He'd lain Jack Booth out against that wall. The dead man was still there. He was moving a little, a fact which made one of Yakima's ribs—one close to his heart—turn cold.

He held the lamp a little higher, scowling into the weak watery yellow light it shed against the base of the western wall. Sure enough, Booth was shuddering as though deeply chilled.

His head lay very close to the wall's base, farther over than Yakima had carelessly positioned it. It almost looked as though Booth were pressing an ear to a crooked crack in the wall to eavesdrop on doings on the other side. The rest of his body lay slack but quivering slightly, his stiffening fingers trembling atop his thighs.

His open eyes dully reflected the lamp's glow. It was an eerie sight to see—a dead man trembling like that, his eyes glowing between lazy lids.

It was as though the body were housing a demon of some kind.

Yakima's throat went dry. His tongue swelled. His boots grew heavy.

The curse.

Could it be that the old Apache witch had...?

He let the thought trail off. It was too impossible as well as terrifying to dwell on. Still, he stared down in silent horror at the dead man's quivering carcass, his heart quickening.

Then the shuddering stopped.

There was a scratching noise down somewhere near the body. The shuddering started again. Stopped. Started again. It stopped and was replaced with the scratching sound.

Yakima drew a deep breath and felt a smile tug at his face. "Oh...Christ!"

His heart slowing with relief, his muscles relaxing, he let the lamp hang from its wire and strode forward. He unsnapped the keeper thong from over his Colt's hammer, drew the big piece from its holster, clicked the hammer back, aimed at the crack in the wall just above Jack Booth's broad nose, and fired.

The cannonading detonation was followed by a sharp, loud yip from the other side of the adobe wall. The yip was followed closely by the patter of four padded feet running away, the patter dwindling quickly. The bullet had blasted a large chunk out of the thick adobe, widening the crack, but hadn't gone all the way through.

Wolf and Emma's buckskin whickered loudly. One of them kicked its stall with a sharp wooden thud.

Yakima gave a snort as he holstered the smoking Colt. The fox had returned. He snapped the keeper thong over the .44's hammer, chuckling. "Got a feeling he won't be back tonight, Jack. You can rest easy now, pard. I'll get you back to Apache Springs in one piece, get you fitted for a wooden overcoat."

The fox had likely smelled Booth seasoning inside the stable. Apparently, it had stuck its pointed snout far enough through the crack that it had gotten its teeth on Booth's shirt collar, and was tugging on the dead man while pausing occasionally to try to dig in under the wall.

Until Yakima had shown it the error of its ways.

Yakima grabbed his bedroll up off his saddle and tossed it onto a lump of old moldering hay on the floor, unrolling it. "Hope you don't mind a little company tonight, Jack. I also hope you don't snore. I haven't had a good night's sleep in..."

He let his voice trail off as running footsteps rose from outside the stable, from the direction of the shack. The footsteps grew louder before stopping just outside, and Emma said, "Yakima?"

"What?"

"Are you all right?"

"Fine," he grumbled.

"What was the shootin' about?"

"The fox came back, was nibblin' on ole Jack."

"Oh," was all Emma said. But she didn't leave. She stood out there silently for nearly a minute before she said in a voice pitched with intimacy, "Yakima?"

He lay down on his bedroll and turned his saddle over to use the underside as a pillow. "What?"

She nudged the stable door, which he'd barred from inside. "Let me in."

"No."

Another short pause before she said more softly, her intimate voice laced with urgency, "You know you want to."

"Yes, I do. But I'm not gonna do it. Go on back to the shack."

"Come on."

"Go to bed, Emma."

"I want to come to bed with you, Yakima."

"No."

"Come on."

"No."

Another brief pause. She whacked her fist against the door. Hard. "Let me in!"

Yakima lay back against his saddle and ground his molars.

"Let me in, Yakima, damn you!"

He didn't say anything. He was fighting off his desire for the beautiful young woman. Why, he asked himself? Because he still thought that maybe he had a chance with her sister?

Maybe deep down beneath just his loins talking he really didn't want her despite the wildcat that she was. *The wildcat in the sack* that she was. That's how much he wanted her sister. For real and true.

"Yakima?" Very soft and pleadingly, her ripe lips held up very close to the stable door. "Just for tonight? No one else will never know."

He drew a deep breath and stared at the cracked ceiling in the shadows above the lamp's reach.

"Goddamn you!" Emma screeched.

She pummeled the door with her fists and her boots. She beat it till he thought she was either going to break her hands or feet or the door itself. Finally, the clattering stopped. She wheeled and strode furiously back toward the shack, her crunching footsteps fading until he heard her boots on the stoop and then the shack's door slamming shut.

Yakima got up and blew out the lamp. He lay back down and curled up on his side.

"'Night, Jack."

***

Another storm front moved in the next morning just before dawn, soaking the desert and filling the arroyos.

The bad weather kept Yakima, Emma, and Rusty Tull from leaving the cabin till early afternoon. Instead, they sat in the old adobe shack playing three-handed poker for matchsticks while a stripe-tailed scorpion climbed about the cracked walls and the rain streamed from the eaves and drip-drip-dripped through the leaky roof and into a tin pot on the floor.

Yakima and Emma glowered across the table at each other, and Rusty eyed them each warily, like two wildcats meeting up in the same arroyo, tails curled.

They didn't ride into Apache Springs until early evening, the streets already clotted with drunken miners and prospectors and the track layers still in town to spend the last of the wages they'd received when the final ties and rails were laid, the last spikes hammered into the main street of Apache Springs.

The three riders, worn out and weary of each other's companionship, rode somberly toward the Conquistador

Inn though Yakima pulled up short when the Rio Grande Kid hailed him from out front of Cleve Dundee's grand and rollicking Busted Flush Saloon. The Kid wore the town marshal's badge on the upper left flap of his brown leather vest. He'd been keeping it nice and shiny. He had a double-barrel shotgun resting on his right shoulder.

The big older man scowled up in pleasant surprise. "I thought...I thought you'd done hauled your freight out of—"

"Just tyin' up some loose ends," Yakima said.

The Kid's eyes were on the dead man lying belly down over the saddle of the horse Yakima was trailing. "Who's that?"

"Jack Booth."

"Oh, he works for Kosgrove, don't he?"

"That's who I'm headin' to see right now."

Yakima nudged Wolf forward, after Emma and Rusty, who'd gone ahead, riding double on Emma's buckskin, but stopped when the Kid said, "Marsh...er, I mean, Yakima?"

"What is it?"

"Bad news about Julian Barnes."

"Tell me."

"He didn't make it."

"Ah, shit."

"There's more news about him."

"Hold it for now, will ya, Kid? I'll come over to the

office after I see Kosgrove."

"All right—see ya, then." The Kid watched Yakima ride on up the street, along the right side of the silver rails that glowed in the yellows and umbers of the street-side lamps and burning oil pots. The Kid yelled hopefully, "You gonna stay in town, after all, Yak?"

"No," Yakima grunted.

He reined up in front of the Conquistador. Emma's horse stood tied to one of the three crowded hitchracks. Rusty stood beside the horse as though wondering what he should do, where he should go. Emma was just then striding quickly up the Conquistador's broad front steps, a determined set to her shoulders, chaps flapping about her shapely thighs.

Yakima swung down from Wolf's back and tied the stallion as well as Booth's horse to the same hitchrack at which Emma had tied her buckskin.

"Come on, kid," Yakima said as he strode past Rusty. "Take a load off."

"What're you talkin' about? I don't got a room here. Hell, I don't have a room anywhere." Rusty was hurrying to keep up with Yakima taking the porch steps two at a time, weaving around the nightly revelers, some with gaudily clad doves clinging to their arms.

"I still have a room here," Yakima told the young man on his heels, raising his voice to be heard above the din.

"You can stay in it till you find something else. I won't be needing it much longer. I'll make the arrangements."

Rusty's quick, wide-eyed glance took in the breadth and opulence of the place, and he said, "I don't...I don't have near enough money to stay in a place like this. Fact, I don't have any money at all!"

"You don't need any money." Yakima stopped and smiled dubiously at the young man. "I know the lady who runs the place." He winked.

16

Yakima continued up the veranda steps and into the Conquistador, Rusty on his heels.

He stopped when he saw Emma talking to Julia, who stood near the bar, a tray of empty bottles and glasses in her hands. The two continued speaking then Julia turned once toward Yakima, looked away, then jerked her gaze back to the tall half-breed standing in the doorway, the diminutive redhead flanking him.

Julia's eyes blazed.

Emma stopped talking and followed her sister's eyes. A faint expression of satisfaction shaped itself on the younger sister's lips. She walked away from Julia and over to Yakima and Rusty. She continued on past them, saying, "Pa's out at the house. I'm headin' there right now."

"Save your horse," Yakima said, his gaze on Julia, her gaze still on him.

"I'll put him up in the livery and rent a fresh one. I gotta know Pa's intentions."

"Too dark," Yakima absently objected.

"I know the trail." She strode quickly down the steps and into the street choked with clumps of drunken day's-end revelers.

Yakima walked over to Julia. She turned away from him, set the tray on the bar, and walked around behind it. As she came back up the other side toward the tray, she said, "Did you and my sister have a good time out in the desert?" Her eyes glinted fire. "Where'd you spend last night? The Javelina Bluffs again?"

"Nothin' happened between us. I made sure of it."

Julia tossed the empty bottles into a bucket on the floor, flaring her nostrils as she did so, her cheeks flushed with anger. "Tough fight?"

"Never mind that."

"I thought you were leaving town."

"Soon."

Julia stopped what she was doing and stared at him obliquely. "Really?"

Yakima glanced at Rusty standing beside him but gazing around at the game trophies mounted on the walls, which were papered in gold-leaf against spruce green above the varnished walnut wainscoting. "Listen, I got a kid here who needs a room for a while. His

179

family is layin' dead out in the desert, an' he doesn't have any money."

Julia tossed another bottle into the bucket with a noisy clatter. "I'm neither an orphanage nor a charity."

"I'm paid up through the month. He can have my room."

"Are you vouching for his character?"

Yakima chuckled without humor. "All I can tell you it's a helluva lot better than mine."

"I don't doubt it a bit."

In the corner of his eye, Yakima saw a familiar face. He turned to look directly across the bar at Kosgrove's dapper English business partner, John Clare Hopkins.

The man was drinking brandy from a snifter and smoking a stout cigar. He gave Yakima a dubious smile and raised the snifter in salute though there was a hard, baleful look in his dark eyes set beneath heavy, groomed brows. Those eyes bored into Yakima. A gold pinky ring winked in the light from a chandelier behind him, before the entrance to the Puma Den.

Pouring a drink for a customer near Yakima, Julia regarded Rusty Tull.

"He seems a tad milder than you. I bet he doesn't even go on four-day rampage-benders, howling like a gut-shot wolf." She glanced sidelong at Yakima.

His ears warmed. "Have someone haul water up to my room so the poor kid can have a bath, will you? And a good meal?"

"Anything else?" Julia said with sarcasm.

"That'll work for now."

She set the bourbon in front of the customer and scooped the man's coins off the bar. She glanced at Rusty and then at Yakima. "I'll take care of him."

"There is one more thing. He could use a job. Think about it, will ya?"

Julia pulled her mouth corners down, nodding. She studied Yakima with somber fondness. She found it touching that he'd taken the kid under his wing. "I'll see what I can do."

"Thanks. I have to talk to the new town marshal."

Yakima turned away but turned back when she called his name.

Julia gazed at him, her eyes unreadable, impenetrable. She shook her head. "Nothing." She mopped at the bar with a towel. "You're, uh...you're leaving, then?"

Yakima glanced at John Clare Hopkins again. The man wore a full-on scowl now, regarding Yakima through his billowing cigar smoke.

Yakima returned his gaze to Julia. "Soon."

He waited for her to tell him to stay though he didn't know how he'd have responded if she had. They were doomed any way you looked at it. Still, it was hard to just ride away from a woman like this. It had been hard to bury Faith, but he'd had no choice in that deal, since he'd ultimately been unable to save her from Thornton's men.

Julia, however, was still living and breathing. Her life would go on without him in it, and the thought battered him with a sudden anguish.

How could his go on without her in it?

When she dropped the towel on the bar and turned away to tend Rusty, not offering Yakima the words he wanted to hear, he moved away from the bar again and headed back out of the Conquistador and into the street. She thought that he and Emma had been together again, in the Javelina Bluffs. He supposed they had in a way, every bit as much as if he'd let her into the stable the previous night, for he'd had to fight his desire like a rabid puma.

He was about to cross the railroad tracks when a man stepped out from a small group of burly imbibers and grabbed his arm. He was nearly as big as Yakima. A track layer, Yakima thought. The man's eyes danced with drunken belligerence but a mocking smile shaped his mouth as he said, "You half-breed son of a bitch!"

He brought a fist up from his knees, bunching his lips with the effort. He didn't get the hand level with his shoulder before Yakima slammed his right fist into the man's jaw. It was a stunning, unexpected blow. It sent the man stumbling backwards and unclenching his fist as he threw his arms out for balance.

The man had crawled Yakima's hump at the wrong time. He might have seen that Yakima no longer wore the badge on his shirt, but the half-breed was a small corral bursting at the rails with big, angry stallions just then. His green eyes blazing with silent fury and pent up frustration, Yakima followed the man back toward the Conquistador, pummeling his shocked, inebriated opponent with resounding lefts and rights, battering his head like a blacksmith toiling over an anvil.

In less than a minute, maybe less than thirty seconds, the man lay wheezing in the street, spitting blood from his smashed lips. Blood oozed from both of his torn brows. Two broken teeth were pasted by blood to his chin whiskers.

"Jesus Christ, Marshal," complained one of the man's friends gathered loosely around them in wide-eyed shock. "You're gonna *kill* ole Whitey!"

Yakima straightened. He glanced at his fists, both sets of knuckles scraped and bloody though whose blood it was he couldn't tell in the weak, guttering light from the oil pots. He plucked his hat off the street, brushed it off, set it on his head. He cursed, swung away from his groaning opponent, whom his friends were now tightly surrounding, and brushed his fists across his trousers.

A young boy who stood little higher than Yakima's cartridge belt walked up to the former marshal of

Apache Springs. He was one of the street urchins whose numbers had been growing along with the rest of the population and whose ilk had no curfew but lingered out after dark in hopes of landing an odd job or two for badly needed pocket jingle. Such boys' parents were largely absent or in no condition, due to alcohol or drug addiction, to adequately tend their offspring, so such children fended for themselves.

The boy spat a wad of snoose to one side, sniffed two streams of dirty snot into his nose, yanked his too-large pants up on his narrow hips and said, "Nice bare-knuckle work, Marshal. I'll tend Wolf and the fresh beef for a dollar."

"Your prices are goin' up, Lonnie."

"Prices are goin' up all over town." Lonnie stuck out a dirty little hand, palm up and with a cockeyed grin on his lightly freckled face.

Yakima flipped the kid a dollar. "Rub 'em down good."

Lonnie stuck out his hand again. "That'll be an extra quarter."

Yakima raised a brow.

The boy said, "It's the railroad! What should I do with the beef?"

"Lay him out in the hay. I'll come for him first thing in the morning."

"Gramps says dead men attract vermin." Gramps

Dawson owned the livery barn.

"Tell Gramps to kiss my…" Yakima paused, reconsidered, and said, "Tell Gramps I'll come for him first thing in the morning."

Lonnie's customarily sober features broke into a snaggle-toothed grin.

Yakima flipped the kid another fifty cents and told him to keep the change. While Lonnie led Wolf and the claybank away, Yakima crossed the tracks and continued east to the marshal's office where the Kid stood waiting for him on the raised wooden gallery, his ubiquitous Greener perched on his shoulder. A half-smoked quirley jutted from a corner of his mouth.

"How's business?" Yakima asked him.

"All the cells are occupied, and it's still early. We're gonna need another jail soon or we'll have to just shoot all the drunken brawlers, since we won't have no place to house 'em."

"Suits me." Yakima walked up onto the stoop and ladled water from the rain barrel over each set of knuckles.

"Whose face did you rearrange?" the Kid asked.

"Whitey Ugstead."

The Kid gave a dry chuckle then turned to walk through the jailhouse's half-open door. "Come on inside. I know you ain't officially the marshal no more, but I'm in a pickle of what to do with this."

Yakima waved his burning knuckles in the dry air and followed the Kid into the jailhouse. All four cells along the back wall were indeed occupied. Most of the prisoners—there appeared around nine—were sleeping and snoring. One Mexican was strumming a mandolin. He saw Yakima and gave a cordial nod as he continued strumming.

"What did Lopez do?" Yakima asked the Kid.

"Started a fight with a gringo by pissin' in the man's beer."

"He cheated me at cards, Marshal Henry," explained Hector Lopez then continued strumming. "So, I salted his beer when he went to the privy." He smiled beneath his thick, drooping black mustache.

"That'll teach him." Yakima turned to the Kid. "What you got for me?"

The older man had sagged down in the chair behind the desk and pulled a sheet of paper out of a drawer. He unfolded the page, set it on the desk, and smoothed it out with his thick hands before turning it toward Yakima. "Read that. Before he died, Julian Barnes dictated this note to Doc Sutton, and signed it."

The Kid pulled the note back, frowning up at Yakima. "Can you read?"

Yakima gave a snort. "When the chips are down I can sound it out."

"Doc had to tell me what it said." The Kid chuckled

with self-deprecation.

Yakima slid the notepaper toward him. There was a single sentence in blue-black ink, in a flowing, college-educated hand. The gawdy cursive was in stark contrast to the bluntness and brevity of the sentence itself:

"I was killed by Hugh Kosgrove." It was signed by Julian Barnes in a shaky, spidery scrawl, the 's' in Barnes's name badly smeared, as though the dying man had used the last of his strength to sign the note, his hand collapsing at the end.

"What do you make of it?" the Kid asked, frowning up at Yakima.

Yakima straightened, shrugged. "None of Kosgrove's enemies have ever lived very long. But that might just be a dying man tryin' to take out a blood enemy with his last gasp."

"Doc says a dying man's testament is bond in a court of law."

"Yeah, well..." Yakima swung around and headed for the door. "Good luck getting Hugh Kosgrove in a court of law. He stopped at the threshold and glanced back at the Kid. "I got bigger fish to fry with Kosgrove."

"Oh? What's that?"

"He sicced a couple of bushwhackers on me and Rusty Tull."

"Why?"

"That's just what I'm gonna ask him when I ride out of here tomorrow mornin'."

Yakima went out. Behind him, the Kid rushed over to the door and yelled, "What about this Julian Barnes affair?"

"Folks know what happens when you mess with Kosgrove," Yakima said. Smiling, he glanced back at the older man once more. "Besides, it ain't none of my business. You're the one with the badge on your vest. It looks right good there, too—if you don't mind the compliment?"

The Kid stared down at the badge on his lumpy chest, ran his thumb across it. "I reckon it does, don't it? Been keepin' a shine on it." He looked at Yakima again, his features grave, troubled. "Sure weighs heavy, though."

Yakima heard yelling to the east and saw Galveston Penny hazing a couple more drunks at rifle point toward the jailhouse.

Yakima glanced up at the Kid again. "It does at that."

He swung around and continued walking. He needed a thick steak and a pile of beans then a long night's sleep. The stable would suffice. He'd saddle Wolf at first light at ride out to powwow with Kosgrove.

17

Since the supper hour had passed, the Bon Ton Restaurant had several empty tables for Yakima to pick from.

He chose one in the room's front corner, opposite the door. He'd made enough enemies that it was always wise to sit with his back to a wall. A corner was even better. This way he had a good view of the entire long, deep room lit by several hanging, sooty oil lamps.

The Bon Ton was his favorite place in town not only because the food was good but because, despite the name, there was nothing pretentious or expensive about it, which wasn't something you could say about the Conquistador. The food over there wasn't bad, but it was nothing compared to what the old Swedish cooks, husband and wife, scraped off the big iron grill in the Bon Ton's rear kitchen and was served by their two stout and unfriendly daughters, Helga and Linny.

Yakima's stomach was growling like a dog with a bone. He was weak with hunger. He hadn't had more than a few bites in days, not since before his humiliating display with several bottles in the jailhouse, and he felt as empty as a dead man's boot.

He ordered from the unsmiling, blue-eyed Linny a giant steak and a plate of beans with four eggs and chili sauce laid over the top, with carrots and tomatoes on the side, and a basket of the Swedes' grainy brown bread, which was the best bread he'd ever tasted anywhere. Apple cobbler with freshly whipped cream rounded out the deal, and when it all came, he nearly fainted from the enticing fragrances rising with the steam off the four heaping platters.

"Anyt'ing else, nay?" Linny asked, refilling his coffee cup with coal-black coffee then scribbling out the bill and slapping it down on the table.

"Nay," Yakima said.

Linny never made eye contact with him. Yakima suspected she didn't cotton to stooping to serve a man with Indian blood, even when that man had been the town marshal. Normally, that would get Yakima's neck in a hump, but since there was something touching in the unattractive and ungainly girl's shyness, and the food was good, he never got worked up about it.

Besides, he wouldn't be strapping on the feed bag in

this town much longer. He'd be pulling his picket pin soon, maybe spend the winter a little farther west, around the Arizona-California border, possibly along the sandy shores of the Sea of Cortez.

Yakima was halfway through his meal, the tender, bloody beef going down like candy, when five men entered the place in a single group. What caught Yakima's eye about them, through the smoke still lifting from his food, was that they were better dressed than those who usually dipped their snouts in the Bon Ton's rough-hewn though tasty trough. The problem with good food was that it attracted all kinds, and Yakima had seen unfortunate signs that the Bon Ton was starting to attract three-piece suits now and then, and even a few petticoats and ostrich-plumed picture hats.

What warranted a second glance at this current bunch, however, was that one of them had a familiar face.

"Ah, shit," Yakima grumbled to himself around a mouthful of half-chewed steak and beans.

John Claire Hopkins saw Yakima about the same time Yakima saw Hopkins, who led the four others, similarly dressed in tailored suits and bowler hats, and wearing trimmed facial hair and gold watch chains, into the humble eatery. Only, Hopkins didn't look nearly as surprised as Yakima felt about their unexpected meeting in such an unlikely haunt.

Or…maybe Hopkins had expected to find him here. Yakima had seen a man leave the premises rather quickly after he had taken his seat in the corner. Was the Englishman keeping tabs on him?

Yakima didn't know much about the man except that he was English, had a close business relationship with Hugh Kosgrove, had pecuniary ambitions here in Apache Springs, and that he'd set his hat for Julia. Yakima had a feeling he was about to find out more, for the man, after ushering his friends to a table just beyond Yakima's, down the long room on Yakima's right, sauntered over to Yakima's table, dipping his beringed fingers into the shallow pockets of his silk waistcoat which resided behind a midnight black brocade clawhammer coat with wide, silk-faced lapels.

He stood studying Yakima skeptically for a time, with cool disdain. A blue vein just above his right eyebrow throbbed. It would have been unnoticeable if light from a near, low-hanging lamp, didn't hit it just right.

Yakima continued eating, showing the popinjay, who he didn't much care for, no politeness whatever. He did, however, kick out the chair from the other side of his table and say with a mouthful of the food he was chewing, "Sit down an' take a load off, amigo."

"I'll stand."

Yakima shrugged and continued eating. "Okay, then—

out with it. The stench of your toilet water is interfering with the taste of my meal."

Cheeks flushing slightly, Hopkins glanced toward his friends, who'd taken a table just beyond the empty table to Yakima's right. Returning his flinty gaze to Yakima, the dandy said, "Don't pester Julia again. Leave her alone."

"I didn't realize I was pestering her."

"Bringing some young Confederate desert rat into the Conquistador is an embarrassment to her as well as to her father. Having her give him a room and a bath and supper in his bedroom is merely making a mockery of what she does…and what the Conquistador is all about. The boy is filthy, he smells bad, and he can't even speak proper English."

Yakima stopped eating to look up at the man over a forkful of food he held in front of his mouth. "You done?"

"No, I'm not done. I want you personally to stop hovering around her, as well. She is too good for you. You know that, or you should know that. Now understand this—I've asked her to marry me."

Yakima's heart thumped. He manufactured a stony expression, as if the man's words hadn't pierced his thick hide like poison-tipped Apache arrows. "You did, did you?"

"Yes, I did."

"What'd she say?"

"She said yes, of course."

Yakima paused. The food inside him no longer felt as good as it had only a moment before. "I don't believe you."

Hopkins raised his voice for the benefit of his friends sitting nearby. "I don't care what you believe, Henry. But rest assured, Julia and I will soon be married. And I want you to leave her alone. Understand?"

"I'm sorry, Hopkins, but I don't take orders from you. Hell, I don't even like you. You see—me an' Julia got us a special relationship." Yakima's wolf was on a very short leash now, and he had to suppress the urge to climb up out of his chair and pummel the man just as he'd done to Whitey Ugstead an hour ago. "She likes how I treat her, and I like how she treats me. An' just as soon as I'm done with this right tasty an' fillin' meal, I'm gonna go over there an' curl her toes for her...just the way she likes 'em curled. If your room is anywhere near hers, you'd best move. I'm afraid our caterwaulin' will keep you awake most of the night."

Yakima grinned jeeringly then shoved the forkful of food into his mouth and resumed chewing.

Hopkins' cheeks turned bright red. He cast a quick, embarrassed glance at his friends, who were looking toward him and Yakima. He closed his hands over the back of the chair before him, squeezing till his knuckles turned white beneath his several rings. "You big, unwashed, uncouth, savage fool." He'd said the words softly but slowly and in a voice as hard as his eyes. "You don't really think I would allow that to happen, do you? Now that she's promised herself to me…?"

Yakima grinned despite the giant fist squeezing his heart. "We'll see, I reckon."

"Yes." It was Hopkins turn to grin. "We will see."

Shaking his head disdainfully, he turned away, strode over to his friends' table, and sat down. The group immediately began talking and chuckling in hushed tones. Yakima didn't look at them though he felt their eyes on him. He continued eating, shoveling the food in as though with relish though he felt little of the pleasure he'd felt before. Now he was just eating because he didn't want the English popinjay to know how deeply his words had bit him.

When he was finished, with feigned, exaggerated leisure, he scrubbed his napkin across his mouth, belched loudly, shoved his plate away, donned his hat, and rose from his chair. He belched again, keeping his eyes off Hopkins and his toney friends, and dropped some coins onto the table. He sauntered to the door, letting his spurs rake loudly across the floor, and headed outside. Quickly, he stepped to the right of the door and leaned back against the wall, drawing a deep, slow, calming breath.

At least, he'd intended the breath to be calming. It

did anything but calm him. The world looked a little cockeyed. His well-filled guts ached, as though he'd eaten poison. He drew another breath and then started walking along this dark side-street.

Well, she'd accepted the limey bastard's hand in marriage. Why shouldn't she have? The man had money. He'd keep her living high on the hog. What kind of life could Yakima have given her? The actual answer was probably several steps below the life that Lon Taggart had given her.

Taggart had been the marshal here before Yakima. In fact, Yakima had tracked and killed Taggart's killers. Julia had fallen in love with Taggart despite the fact the man had been a lowly public servant. Despite the fact that her father had forbidden her to do so.

She had a habit of defying her father. Both of those women did though they couldn't have been much more unalike otherwise. Julia had fallen in love with Yakima—again despite her father's having forbid their being together.

Maybe it was high time she listened to the old man. She'd have a better life that way, though whether or not Yakima was going to leave Kosgrove alive tomorrow was a matter he hadn't yet decided. If the man had sent Booth to that canyon, he was a cold-blooded killer. He might have killed Barnes, as well. Someday, somehow, Kosgrove needed to be stopped.

After he'd staggered around the north side of town, wandering aimlessly, drunk on the knowledge that Julia was no longer his though he'd doubted she'd ever been his in the first place, and knowing that she would be better off with the limey son-of-a-moneyed-bitch, Hopkins, he recovered his bearings and headed for the livery barn. His blather about going over to the Conquistador and throwing the blocks to Julia had been just that—blather.

He was done with her, just as she was done with him, and rightfully so.

He regretted what he'd said to Hopkins. His stupid words, spawned by his typically uncontrolled rage, wouldn't help her at all. They might even hurt her in Hopkins's eyes though even the stupid limey sonofabitch likely knew he couldn't do any better than Julia Kosgrove. What man could? Still, waving her and Yakima's sex life in front of the man had been stupid and cruel and he shouldn't have done it.

What he really needed was to get his raggedy ass out of here. It had been time for a while, and now it was really time. All he could do here was lay waste to the place, hurt the woman he loved. Hurt her sister, too, whom he didn't love. At least, not in the same way he loved Julia.

What he loved about Emma was her wildness. In that way, she reminded him of Faith. But she wasn't Faith.

While Emma enjoyed making love with Yakima, and only God knew how much he'd enjoyed making love with her, she'd come between him and the real thing—Julia.

Between him and real love.

But, then, he'd let her do it. He'd let her use him as a pawn against her sister with whom she'd been in competition with for most of her life. The really crazy thing was that Yakima knew that deep down the sisters actually loved each other. He'd gotten in *their* way.

What a complicated mess!

But so much of life was, he'd come to realize...

That said, the best thing he could do for Julia and for Emma was to haul his freight out of Apache Springs once and for all, and he would do that just as soon as he talked to Kosgrove about that bushwhacking in the canyon. He couldn't let that go. He had to know why Kosgrove had sent those bushwhackers after him. Why he'd killed the Bundrens, not that they were any great loss.

Also, he wanted to know Kosgrove's intentions regarding the treasure trove in the church. There probably wasn't much he could do about them, but he had to know before he left.

He made his way to the livery barn, entering through the man-door beside the big stock doors, and stumbled around the semi-darkness inside, looking for the stable in which Wolf had been housed. He was glad the cranky liveryman, Gramps Dawson, wasn't around. He was likely off getting drunk with the rest of Apache Springs.

In a few minutes, he was sacked out in the loft. He was sleeping the sleep of the dead until he was awake and he heard the click of a gun being cocked. It was his own thumb cocking his own gun as he aimed it straight out before him.

He'd heard something.

It came again—a wooden creak and a soft thud. Someone was climbing the loft ladder. Yakima squeezed the revolver's neck as he slid the gun to his right.

A woman's soft voice pitched with intimacy. "Yakima?"

Yakima depressed the Colt's hammer. "Ah, hell."

18

"Go away, Julia. I'm dead-dog tired."

The wooden creaks continued. He saw her shadow rise from the ladder's hole to his right, along the base of the barn's south wall.

"How in the hell did you find me?" he asked as she moved slowly over to where he'd laid out his soogan in a pile of fresh hay.

"It wasn't too hard. You weren't in your room and you weren't over at the jail office. You'd given up your badge, so I figured you weren't working. I knew you'd be here."

Somehow, she must have learned that when he couldn't sleep in his room at the Conquistador, he often came out here to sleep in the loft. He always slept better in the silence of a big barn, with the animals and the smells of hay and leather and wool and the musky aroma of the horses themselves.

He rose up to lean on an elbow. "What the hell are you doing here?"

She stood before him, her lithe figure wrapped in a shawl against the evening's chill. Her curvy female figure was mostly a silhouette, but the starlight angling through the two loft windows, one each end of the barn, played in her pinned-up hair.

"I don't have any idea."

"Hopkins said he popped the question."

"He did."

"He said you'd accepted."

"I did."

"So...what're you doin' here?"

"Like I said, I have no idea." She paused. He heard her draw a breath then swallow. "All I know that under this dress, I'm not wearing a damn thing."

She dropped the shawl. She reached down and pulled the simple house dress up and over her head. She let it fall to the floor, then kicked out of her deerskin slippers. Staring down at him, the starlight limning the slow, gentle curves of her breasts, she reached up and unpinned her hair, letting it tumble down around her shoulders.

Yakima's heart was beating quickly against his sternum, and his throat was going dry.

She knelt before him, placed her hand gently against

his cheek, sliding a lock of his long, black hair behind his ear.

He kicked out of his boots and pulled her toward him, burying his face in the deep valley between her breasts.

"Oh, Yakima," she said, wrapping her arms around his head, drawing her taut against him. "What am I going to do without you?"

***

"Damn, Jack—you're gettin' ripe."

Yakima glanced over his right shoulder at the cadaver riding belly down over the claybank. It had been relatively cool in the wake of the last two storms, so Yakima hadn't detected a scent from Jack Booth's stiffening corpse until earlier this morning, when he'd back-and-bellied the man over his saddle again, for Jack's last ride out to his employer's place of residence.

He'd leave Booth with Kosgrove, have the man who'd gotten him killed see to his internment.

It was nearly ten in the morning, with the sun high, and Jack was getting even riper.

"Sure wouldn't want to be the one to have to dig your grave," Yakima said as he crested a ridge then started down the other side.

There was a shrill banging sound as what could only

have been a bullet hammered the top of a boulder to his right. He jerked back on Wolf's reins, and both the stallion and Jack Booth's gelding gave indignant whinnies as the crack of the rifle that had fired the bullet reached the bottom of the canyon.

Yakima fought his instinct to reach for the Yellowboy snugged down in its scabbard to his right. Instead, he kept a taut hold on Wolf's reins and on the lead rope of Booth's mount, and held his place there on the canyon floor.

He looked around at the two sloping ridges rising to either side of him. Both were strewn with rock and chaparral. He wasn't sure where the bullet had come from. He had a feeling he'd know in a minute, after whomever had fired it had let him sit anxiously, waiting...

Sure enough, after nearly a minute had passed, a man's voice caromed down from the ridge on his right, lazy with insolence:

"What do you want, breed?"

The man—one of Kosgrove's trouble-shooters—had glassed him and recognized him. Yakima had expected as much. You couldn't get very close to Kosgrove's layout, the lion's den, so to speak, without being thoroughly vetted.

Kosgrove was a wealthy and powerful man. Like most wealthy and powerful man, that wealth and power came with a good bit of paranoia. He kept a small army of men around him, to protect him from those who might want to separate him from his wealth and power.

Or who might want to see him about a reckoning he was due…

"Wanna powwow with the big chief," Yakima yelled up the ridge on his right.

Silence.

Shortly, two riders appeared, each weaving his way down the ridges—one on his left, the other on his right. The man on his left rode with his Winchester resting on his shoulder. The other held his rifle across his saddle-bows. The clacking of their horses' hooves grew steadily until Yakima could also hear the squawking of the saddles and the soft clicking of their bridle chains.

The man on the right reached Yakima first, halting his strawberry roan about twenty feet up the ridge and scowl-ing down from beneath his weathered, funnel-brimmed hat. The other arrived a few seconds later—a rangy black man wearing a creamy white Boss of the Plains Stetson. A black cheroot angled out one corner of his full-lipped mouth, the smoke slithering out his broad, black nostrils.

"Who's that?" he asked, when both he and the other man had considered the dead man on the horse behind Yakima.

"Jack Booth."

"What the hell'd you kill Jack for?" asked the white man on Yakima's right, his voice taut with anger. He furled his brows, which nearly met over the bridge of his nose, and swung his Winchester carbine out one-handed, aiming it at Yakima's belly.

"To keep him from killing me," Yakima told him, mildly.

The black man looked at the white man. "Boss ain't gonna like that."

"No, he ain't," said the white man, a faint delight in his gaze. Turning to Yakima, he said, "You wanna see Kosgrove? All right. Let's go see Kosgrove." He canted his head to his right, indicating the trail ahead.

The black man scowled at Yakima and then angrily flicked his black-gloved hand at a fly buzzing around his face.

Yakima nudged Wolf ahead, jerking on the pack horse's lead rope.

His chaperones following closely behind him, keeping their rifles trained on his back, he passed a broad, deeply rutted trail that, from a previous trek out here, Yakima knew led to the Conquistador Mine. He continued along the main trail that followed a broad wash. He swerved sharply left and climbed up and out of the wash and into another, secondary canyon fingering off from the main one.

He and his chaperones climbed a broad, low bench and then another, even higher bench. Spreading out across the broad clearing in the desert before him, Yakima saw what appeared to be a Mexican *hacienda* complete with brightly whitewashed adobe barns, stables, and pole corrals, including a round stone breaking corral with a snubbing post at its center.

Last, a sprawling, low, Spanish-style *casa* boasted a broad, wrought-iron gate with the name *KOSGROVE*.

Yakima and his chaperones reined up before the wrought-iron gate in the courtyard wall as a man stepped through it, frowning curiously, holding a wooden water bucket with a ladle sticking out of it. The man was a tall, lean Indian with long, silver-streaked black hair and an age-wizened face. He wore a black suitcoat and string tie as well as fringed buckskin breeches and fancily beaded moccasins.

A red sash encircled his lean waist.

"Marshal Henry," said Three Moons, Kosgrove's houseman, who spoke English as flawlessly as any white man. In fact, he spoke better English than most of the white men Yakima had known. As the servant's eyes strayed to the packhorse, he said, "To what do we owe the honor?"

"Says he come to powwow with the big chief," Yakima's black chaperone answered for him, his tone not so vaguely sarcastic.

"Who's out there, Three?" Hugh Kosgrove's distinctive voice had risen from behind the wrought-iron gate.

Now the short, barrel-shaped man appeared, stepping out from behind some shrubbery wearing a white silk shirt, corduroy slacks, and red suspenders. He had a mud-encrusted trowel in his hand, and he appeared sweating and out of breath. He and the Indian must have been doing some gardening in the patio, which Yakima remembered from his last visit had been carefully tended.

"We have a visitor—the Apache Springs lawman," said Three Moons, keeping his mildly amused, almond-shaped, inky-black eyes on Yakima.

A faint smile curved his lips. An oblique one.

Yakima remembered from a previous visit that the civilized Apache, who was eastern-educated, always appeared to have much on his mind though he gave little of it away. He would have made a good gambler, though Yakima had never seen him in town and he doubted the man ever left Kosgrove's compound. He seemed very closely allied with his boss, for whom he'd worked for many years, so that he'd almost become a part of the family, a surrogate uncle to both Julia and Emma.

"Ah, shit." Kosgrove waddled out from behind Three Moons, who was nearly as tall as Yakima, and thumbed his white planter's hat back on his broad, red forehead. His frosty blue eyes glowed belligerently in the lens-clear Sierra Estrada light as he took Yakima's measure, scowling. He had a white bandage over the ear that Yakima had notched. "What the hell do you want, you crazy son of a bitch? I oughta have you bullwhipped an' shot!"

Yakima dropped the pack horse's lead rope. "Brought your man home."

"What man?"

"Jack Booth," said Yakima's white escort.

Kosgrove frowned. "Booth?" He blinked incredulously at Yakima. "Why?"

"He bushwhacked me. The other one you sent almost killed your daughter."

"Emma?" Kosgrove inquired, voice raised with worry.

He glanced at Yakima's two escorts. "Lead that horse away from the house. Pee-*you*—what a stench!" The mine owner brushed a hand across his nose, his blue eyes watering. "Bury that body and bury it deep!"

When the escorts had ridden off, the black man leading away Jack Booth's sour carcass, Kosgrove returned his angry, concerned gaze to Yakima. "What the hell happened? What have you and my daughter gotten yourselves mixed up in, and what's all this about some hidden treasure?"

"In a church," added Three Moons.

"Yes, in a church!" said Kosgrove, planting his gloved fists on his hips. "Apparently, this crazy treasure business is what's been keeping her out in the desert for days on end!"

"So, she told you about it." Yakima frowned at the house. "Is Emma here?"

"Yes, she's here, but you sure as hell are not going to see her."

"What are your intentions, Kosgrove? And why in the hell did you send those men to kick me out with a cold shovel—same way you did Collie Bundren and his boys?"

Kosgrove took two angry steps forward, his face red, his eyes ringed with pale, angry circles. "I don't know any Bundrens, but you know why I'd like to see your hide tacked to the wall!"

"You knew about the church, and you wanted to shut me up about it, like you did the Bundrens. What about Emma?"

Kosgrove glowered up at him, speechless. He pivoted on his hips to glance curiously at Three Moons, who merely shrugged his bony shoulders.

Turning back to Yakima, Kosgrove said, "What about her? She came storming in here last night, accusing me of killing these Bundren people and demanding to know what I knew about this...this...this ancient *treasure* in some ancient Spanish *church*"—he flung his arm out and waggled his fingers—"somewhere around here but god knows where. Emma knows!" He chuckled at that. "And now you come riding in with Jack Booth, who, by the way, no longer even works for me. It wasn't Booth I sent for you, you obstinate half-breed son of a bitch. I sent Guzman and Mankiller to snuff your wick an' pickle your ass!"

It was Yakima's turn to scowl in disbelief. He couldn't quite believe what the man had just said. "You sent them?"

"Yes!" the man said as though he were dealing with an idiot.

Yakima cocked his head and narrowed an eye at him. "So, you did have them kill Julian Barnes at Senora Galvez's, after all. Despite what you told me in my office."

"I sure as hell did, yes." The walrus-like Irishman paused, blinked. "Don't tell me you actually believed my blarney!" Kosgrove dug a half-smoked cigar from a pocket of his pants, along with a lucifer, and glanced, grinning in amazement, at Three-Moons, who pulled his mouth corners down and shrugged. "He believed me. Hah! First person who ever believed anything Hugh Kosgrove said, Three. Get a load of that! Write that down on the same wall you marked the girls' heights on, will you?" He laughed again.

Three Moon's broad mouth cracked a smile.

When Yakima just stared at the man, unable to believe even the level of Hugh Kosgrove's gall, Kosgrove said, "You got it right, Henry. I hated that sonofabitch, Barnes. You got it right—he screwed me seven ways from sundown. Nobody screws Hugh Kosgrove and gets away with it. So, I hired those two idiots, Mankiller an' Guzman, knowing they'd take the job because they were too stupid not to, and I told them to kill Barnes and then kill you when you rode out after them."

"Because of Julia."

"Yes. Of course, because of Julia!" Kosgrove had stuck the cigar in his mouth and now he was lighting it, turning it slowly, the flame flaring when he inhaled. "You believed me. I'll be damned!"

He laughed. Then he frowned suddenly, and lowered the cigar, letting another puff roll out from between his thin lips. "I reckon you had the last laugh on that one, though, didn't you? I gotta admit, I felt a might off my feed when I seen you ride back to town with those two devils layin' belly down across their saddles."

Rage was a hot fire burning inside Yakima. As he glared back at the pompous little Irishman, he slid his .44 from its holster and clicked back the hammer, aiming at the man's fat face. "I oughta blow you to hell, you old Irish dog."

"Yeah, well..." Unflustered, Kosgrove looked down at his cigar, rolling it between his short, fat fingers. "I reckon I would, too, if I was in your place. It's a nasty thing—murder." He poked the stogie back into his mouth and gave it a few more thoughtful puffs, studying Yakima shrewdly. "But you won't kill me. You know why I know that?"

Tightly, his index finger drawn snug against the Colt's trigger, Yakima just glared at him.

"Because you love them girls. And you know that, though be the devil I am, they both love their ole pa. You wouldn't hurt them."

Again, Kosgrove puffed the stogie, shaking his head. He smiled and glanced toward his men milling around the outbuildings. "Besides, you wouldn't make it ten feet from the house before my men would shoot you off that handsome black, and draw and quarter you, which I should have them do, anyway"—he fingered the bandage on his left ear—"for that stunt in town the other day. Most men would be dead over that, and you will be too if you don't pull your freight out of here. I hate to go to the trouble of bringing in marshals, but I will, goddamnit! And I'll come to your hanging just to laugh as I watch you dance!"

Yakima continued glaring at the man over the barrel of his cocked Colt. Rage burned behind his eyebrows. He wanted nothing more than to drill a hole through Kosgrove's broad, freckled forehead. If it were any other man, he would have done just that. But he couldn't do it. And the man had been right about why.

Yakima drew a slow, deep breath. He depressed the Colt's hammer, easing it down against the firing pin.

Kosgrove smiled and glanced at Three Moons still standing expressionlessly behind him, on his left. The Indian drew his lips together then turned and walked back into the patio and along the path to the house. Again, it was hard to tell what was on his mind, but he didn't seem to think much of either man—Yakima or his own boss—just now.

"You win, Kosgrove," Yakima said, returning the Colt to its holster. "Someday, you'll get yours, but it's not going to be by me. At least, not here. Not today."

"Yeah, well, I feel the same way about you." Kosgrove gave the stogie another couple of angry puffs, his blue eyes nearly crossing.

Yakima gazed back at the man. He wasn't ready to leave. He might have lost the battle with Kosgrove, but he still had one to go. He just wasn't sure who it was with. "You said Booth no longer worked for you."

"That's right, he didn't."

"Who was he workin' for as of the other day, when I blew out his lamp."

"I don't know. I turned him over to John Clare Hopkins a few months back. John Clare wanted a good couple of men, and I owed the limey devil for helping me out of a financial tight spot, so I gave him several of my ore guards."

Yakima's belly tightened. "Hopkins?"

"That's right."

"What'd he want them for?"

"Ole John Clare's got him some prospects, I understand. He needed muscle to safeguard those prospects. He brought in his brother and some friends, one of who's a mining engineer, and he's thinkin' about opening a gold mine somewhere southwest of Apache Springs. He thinks there's some promising looking geology out that way."

Yakima's belly flipped again. "Promising looking geology out that way, eh?"

"Sure enough. I hope so. Not that he doesn't have enough money, but I hope he gets even richer." Kosgrove stuck the stogie into his mouth again, and smiled as he puffed it, narrowing his eyes with mockery. "For Julia's sake. He's askin' for her hand, don't ya know."

"I know." Yakima looked around. His mind was racing, thinking through what Kosgrove had just told him.

'Promising looking geology', his ass.

He turned again to Kosgrove. "Did you tell Emma what you told me?"

Kosgrove hiked a shoulder. "Yes."

"Where is she?"

"Upstairs. Hasn't come down yet today. She threw a fit, wanted to ride to town, and I locked her in her bedroom. That girl's gone loco. I think she's got sun sickness!" He wagged a finger near his good ear.

"No, she's not." The voice belonged to Three Moons. The Indian was working in the patio.

"No, she's not *what*?" Kosgrove asked gruffly, glancing behind him.

"She's not upstairs, boss."

"What're you talkin' about, Three?"

"I thought you must've let her out earlier," came the Indian servant's voice again. "She rode out of the yard before you were even up this morning."

"Ah, hell," Yakima said. "She headed for town…and Hopkins!"

He reined Wolf around and put the steel to him.

19

Earlier that morning—just after dawn, in fact—Julia Kosgrove stepped onto the staircase that ran up the Conquistador Inn's rear outside wall.

The riser squawked beneath her slippered left foot. She winced and glanced around guiltily, drawing her cape tighter around her head and shoulders. Self-realization dawning on her, she snickered at herself.

Here she was—a twenty-eight-year-old woman sneaking around like a schoolgirl after secretly meeting a boy her parents didn't abide. Well, she was no longer a schoolgirl, but she had met the boy—man, rather—that her father didn't abide, and she couldn't help feeling a schoolgirl's chagrin. She was glad no one else was around at this early hour. Usually, one of the Conquistador's cooks or kitchen boys would be out splitting wood for the breakfast fires, but she fortunately didn't see a soul lurking anywhere near in the morning's deep shadows.

She may not have been a schoolgirl, but it would have looked curious, at the very least, for the Conquistador Inn's manager to be sneaking back into her own building at such an early hour. Curious and downright silly. Of course, she could have been returning from a trip to the privy, but she knew that she was really returning from the livery barn in the loft of which she'd made love with Apache Springs's former town marshal on the very same night that she'd earlier accepted the engagement ring of another man.

John Clare Hopkins.

My god, Julia, she reprimanded herself. What have you done? Rutting like some animal—in a barn, no less!

Moving softly up the staircase, she felt heat rise in her cheeks, and her breasts swell. This time not with embarrassment or anything even close to shame but with that heady, almost ethereal feeling she'd always felt after making love with Yakima. She could still feel his lips pressing against hers, his hands cupping her breasts, his long, hard body toiling against her own.

No one had ever made her feel the way Yakima did. Not Lon, god rest his lovely soul. No one. She had no doubt that John Clare Hopkins would pale in comparison. But what choice had she had but to accept his hand? Yakima was not hers. He would never be hers. He and her own sister had made that very clear. Her father had, as well. Even without those obstacles, Yakima was a stallion no mare could ever tame.

At twenty-eight, Julia was running out of options. Like her father had told her, it was a harsh, cold world. It chewed up and spit out the feeble and impractical. She realized that now. It was only sensible to hitch her star to that of a man who could take care of her. It was a man's world. She knew it was a cynical point of view, but she'd been optimistic and idealistic at one time, and life had done its best to beat such notions out of her...

Still, she couldn't help feeling him, Yakima...still smelling his raw, wild, manly odor...hear his guttural groans when he'd bucked up hard against her and spent himself inside her.

"What am I going to do without you, Yakima?"

She hadn't realized she'd voiced the question aloud as she'd opened the Conquistador's outside third-floor door, but now she heard her voice echo softly in the dim hall's sarcophagal silence. She gave a slight gasp and closed a hand over her mouth, stifling a devilish laugh. She closed the door behind her, latching it very quietly and wincing when she heard the bolt click home, as if anyone else might hear it.

Turning right, she headed off down the dark hall toward her room, relieved at having gotten this far without anyone noticing her silly display but also feeling a heavy sadness wash over her, knowing that the night she'd just spent in Yakima's wild embrace would likely be her last.

She stopped abruptly, heart quickening, when a door latch clicked just ahead and on her left. Her heart beat faster when a door opened and a man stepped out. The man's figure was murky with shadows, but—oh, god, wasn't that John Clare Hopkins's room?

Like a death knell, none other than Hopkins's voice spoke from the shadows concealing his tall, slender figure, "Oh, there you are, darling!"

Julia jerked backward with another, louder gasp, clapping her hand over her mouth once more. Her heart leaped so hard that she felt as though she'd been kicked by a horse.

"What's the matter?" Hopkins stepped out of the shadows and into the dim gray light angling through a window at the hall's far end. "I'm sorry if I frightened you."

"Oh, John." Her heart still racing, Julia lowered her hand. "Yes, uh...yes, you did...you gave me quite a start!" She closed her arms on his breasts with an instinctive effort to conceal the fact she wore nothing beneath the simple cambric house dress she'd worn over to the livery barn.

She chuckled to try to cover her shock at seeing this very man in the hall—the last person in all the world she'd wanted to run into just now. But here he was. Why did she have the chill feeling that the meeting was possibly by design?

The suspicion arose with the fact that he said nothing now but only stared at her, the gradually strengthening gray light touching his face but also casting part of it in shadow. It made one eye glisten eerily.

"Did I catch you at a bad time?" he asked, his voice vaguely menacing.

"What? No." Awkward with self-consciousness, she raised her other arms and lay that hand against her neck. "I mean…what do you mean…?"

"Where've you been, darling?" The toneless voice made her heart flutter.

"I've been…" She frowned. He was fully dressed in his usual tony, carefully arranged garb, and he also wore a crisp black slouch hat. A cigar poked up from the pocket of his left lapel, beside a red silk kerchief thrusting up one sharply folded corner. "What're you doing up so early, John?"

She did not know him to be an early riser.

"I asked you a question?" he said.

She stopped breathing. That gray eye was hard and cold now. She'd never seen his eyes so cold. They'd always only regarded her with a vaguely amused appreciation and adoration. Some might call it obsequiousness. Now he looked not only angry but as though he were harboring a barely restrained rage.

Julia couldn't find her tongue.

"Where've you been?" he asked again, his voice harder and quicker this time, as he took one stiff step forward. Then another step.

Suddenly he was inches away from her. He grabbed her right arm, squeezing painfully. Her mind was slow to catch up to the sudden change in his character, to the fact of his fingers digging into her flesh while his eyes glared down at her sharply, furiously. He was like a dangerous stranger accosting her.

"Don't try to lie," he said. "I know where you were."

"Ow...John...!"

"I know you were with him. I had you followed. Half the town works for me. You can't go anywhere without me knowing...knowing who you're *with*. Yes, I had a man keeping an eye on you. He followed you over to the livery barn. He followed you inside. He...he *heard* what you were doing in the loft with that savage!"

"John..." Her ears ringing, Julia was squirming, trying to loosen his burning grip on her arm. "Please... you're...*hurting me!*"

"You were coupling with that red-skinned heathen on the very night I'd asked you to be my wife!"

"John...I *know*. Please...stop...I *know*...I couldn't help myself. John…I'm sorry, but I *love* him!" She was sobbing now, staring up at the man glaring down at her, twisting her arm until her knees were buckling and she was sliding down the wall toward the floor.

"John!"

He released her arm and she dropped to the floor, curling her legs beneath her, crying, tears rolling down her cheeks. She'd never known such shame. Now she saw what she'd done in the barn for what it was.

Betrayal.

John Clare Hopkins crouched over her, shoving his enraged red face and blazing eyes up close to hers. She could smell brandy on his breath. He was drunk. She could see it in his eyes now, behind his fury. "You're going to be sorry you didn't give me more than a chance, Julia. Very sorry. Soon…very soon…you're going to be very sorry."

He straightened, drew a deep breath, puffing out his chest and continuing to glare down at her. "And so will your father." He stepped backward. "You'll not see me again. I hope you rot…old and alone, running your little whores…in this squalid backwater!"

He turned away then stopped, laughing. "Ah, here's one now!"

Julia peered through her tears around Hopkins' back to see one of the girls—Marlene, a willowy blonde clad now in a thin cotton night dress—standing before him, looking up at him in silent astonishment and horror. She knew John Clare, of course. All the girls did, for he'd been a regular here at the Conquistador for months though Julia didn't think he'd indulged in their pleasures. At least, if he did, she wasn't aware of it. It would have been unseemly for her suitor to have lain with her doxies, though she certainly had no justification for blaming him. But now she realized she knew absolutely nothing about him.

"What are you staring at, you silly little thing?" Hopkins suddenly barked at the girl, like a rabid wolf.

Marlene lurched backward. She was holding two cups of coffee in her hands, but now the coffee in one cup splashed over the hand holding it, and she dropped it. The cup landed with a dull thud on the carpeted floor, the coffee splashing up against the wall.

She glanced at Julia, and said, "I'm s-sorry...I was just looking for Candace Jo...I didn't mean...I didn't mean to..."

"Candace Jo?" asked Hopkins. He laughed again, jeeringly. "You'll find her in my room."

He glanced over his shoulder at Julia, gave her a mocking wink, and then strolled off down the hall, swinging his arms and clapping his hands as though it were just another fine sunny day for a man to enjoy, as if nothing of what had just occurred in the hall had occurred at all.

Marlene set down the other cup of coffee and dropped to a knee beside Julia, "Are you all right, Miss Julia? My god, I've never...*seen* him like that!"

Julia pressed her hands to her face, rubbing away the tears, composing herself. "No," she gulped. "I haven't, either."

"What set him off?"

"I did. It's all my fault."

Marlene stared at her, bewildered. "What? I don't..."

Julia placed a hand on Marlene's arm. "Check his room."

The look the man had given her when he'd winked had added a fresh chill to Julia's bones.

"Check his room," she said again, pressing her fingers into Marlene's arm, pulling herself to her feet, steadying herself with one hand on the wall, one hand on the girl's arm.

"What? Why?"

"Just check his room..." Julia, speaking more to herself than to the young doxie, brushed past Marlene still gaping at her in shock, and strode over to the door of Hopkins' room.

Feeling a nettling apprehension see-saw inside her, making her hesitate with her hand on the doorknob, she finally twisted the knob. She shoved the door open. Frowning, she stepped into the large, opulently furnished suite—the grandest suite in the hotel. Thickening gray light angled through the two tall windows sheathed in long, green, gold-embroidered velvet drapes on the opposite wall.

"Candace Jo...?" Julia said, looking around.

Her gaze went to the bed abutting the papered wall on her left, and she gasped, closing a hand over her mouth.

CANDACE OR JULIA

20

"What is it, Miss Julia?" asked Marlene, stepping into the room behind her.

The young doxie followed Julia's gaze. Marlene also gasped, drawing her shoulders up and sort of hunkering into herself, bringing a hand to her mouth. "*Oh!*"

Stiff with horror, Julia moved forward until she was standing beside the bed, staring down at the naked young brown-haired doxie lying naked before her. Candace Jo's throat was laid open from ear to ear. The bed around her head was awash in the dark crimson of fresh blood. The doxie's eyes were open, and she appeared to still be staring in horror at the man who'd killed her.

There were several cuts and bruises on her face where he'd beaten her. Julia remembered Candace Jo's discolored eye... It had been him. It had been John Clare Hopkins taking out his frustration on the submissive young doxie, whom Hopkins must have paid extra to keep his and Candace's trysts secret. He must have paid the poor girl enough that she'd been willing to overlook the man's abuse.

"That bastard," Julia whispered into the hand she still held over her mouth.

Behind her, Marlene sobbed.

"That bastard," Julia said again, a little louder but with the same disbelief as before. "How could he...?"

But he had. That much was obvious. It was also obvious that John Clare Hopkins was a far different man than the one he'd revealed to Julia. Maybe Julia was different than the person she'd revealed to Hopkins, but she had not murdered an innocent young woman out of sheer spite!

Rage began to mix with Julia's horror and revulsion at what the man had done. She whipped around, turning to Marlene bawling quietly with her bowed head bobbing with emotion. She gently took the girl's arm in her hand and led her into the hall, closing the door behind her.

She didn't know what to say to the girl. Hell, she didn't know what to say to herself. Her mind was awash with mute fury. She left Marlene in the hall and strode quickly to the stairs, no longer caring that she wasn't wearing anything beneath her simple house dress and cape, and that the fact was likely very obvious, especially when she descended the stairs so quickly and jarringly.

Ivor Ingersoll was behind the bar, preparing one of the two coffee urns for the morning's first breakfasters, one of which was coming through the front door as Julia was halfway down the stairs. "Good morning, Miss Julia. You're up awful ear…"

The man let his voice trail off when she saw how fast she was moving, with obvious purpose, and the severe expression on her face. Her long hair, still flecked with bits of hay from the loft, tumbled messily about her shoulders. Julia strode up past the bar, between the bar and the tables arranged along the saloon's right wall…up to the front door, which the town barber, Wilfred Owen, held open for her, the Tucson newspaper tucked beneath his arm.

"Good morning, Julia. And how are you this…" The barber also let the query die on his lips when he saw Julia's obvious state of severe concentration and passionate focus.

He stared at her, frowning, as she strode through the doorway as though a woman in a trance, her face pale, her fiery eyes narrowed. She moved down the veranda's broad steps and into the street, looking around. The sun was on the rise now, and she shaded her eyes with one hand. There were only a few people on the street, which accepted the sun's early, buttery glow, long shadows receding.

The train had pulled into town last night, and the

short combination lay down the street to the east, on her left, near the newly built depot station. The snub-nosed, coal-black engine had already been turned around; it now faced west, the direction it would return to when the train pulled out.

Where was Hopkins? Why had he risen so early? What was he up to? Where was he going?

Her fury roiling inside her, Julia continued to look around for the man who'd killed Candace Jo. The English bastard thought he could get away with anything because he had money, and with money came power, but Julia wanted to let him know that he could not. He *would* not get away with killing a defenseless young girl, even a whore, just to get back at Julia for betraying him.

If only Yakima were here!

He'd ridden out earlier, after he'd slowly dressed in the loft's musky shadows. He'd ridden out to see her father about the man Yakima thought Hugh Kosgrove had sicced on him. Her anger shifted toward the handsome half-breed. Why was she not here now, when he needed her most? Only he could give John Clare Hopkins the licking the killer deserved!

Julia heaved a deep, angry breath and angled across the street to the east, heading for the town marshal's office. Yakima had left the Rio Grande Kid in charge. Julia naturally had some doubts about the Kid's competence, but the older lawman would have to do. He'd fought off a whole horde of angry Chiricahuas only a few days ago, when he'd been transporting a prisoner from Tucson to Apache Springs, so maybe he was more capable than Julia had given him credit for.

She lifted her skirts to cross the tracks and angled sharply left. As she neared the jailhouse, she also neared the train and saw that one of the few cars in the combination was a Wells Fargo Express car. Painted as black as the engine, it was larger than usual, and it appeared of a stouter construction than usual, as well. The only other cars were a passenger coach, a stock car, and the obligatory yellow caboose at the end. These other cars looked shabby by comparison to the well-endowed express car, obviously built for transporting great wealth.

Giving the train only a passing glance, Julia marched up the jail office's rickety wooden front steps. She rapped once on the door then flipped the latch and nudged it open. The big, older man known as the Rio Grande Kid jerked his head up from his chest with a startled grunt, nearly falling over backward in the chair that had once belonged to Julia's now-deceased husband, Lon Taggart. "The Kid" dropped his mule-eared boots from where he'd had them crossed on the desk, to the floor, and reached for the old pistol holstered on his hip.

He forestalled the movement when his wide, sleep-bleary eyes found Julia moving into the room, her jaws hard.

The Kid removed his hand from the old pistol's walnut grips, and said, "Oh, uh...Miss, uh...Miss Kosgr—"

"You must arrest John Clare Hopkins!"

"Wha—*huh*?" Leaning forward in his chair, the Kid blinked as though to clear his eyes. "Arrest *who*, ma'am?"

"John Clare Hopkins!" Julia cried, almost sobbing again, so strong was the emotion triggering through her. "He...*butchered*...one of my girls!"

"Mister *Hopkins* did?"

"You must find him and arrest him...or shoot the son of a bitch!"

The old man flinched a little then turned his head to look at her askance. Julia knew what he must be thinking. He must be wondering if the woman standing before him was really Julia and not her half-feral sister, Emma. She had to admit she was a little bewildered herself by her rather capable impersonation, and by how easily the words had flown from her lips on the wings of raw emotion.

Vaguely, she opined that maybe she and Emma were more alike than either one of them had thought.

"Shoot him?" said the Kid. "Now...why would I do that?"

"I just told you. He killed one of my girls. Slit her throat from ear to ear!"

"Are you sure it was Mister Hopkins?"

"Yes. I found Candace Jo in Hopkins's room."

"Oh. Boy." The big, fleshy-faced, large-bellied man heaved himself out of the chair, making it creak as he did so. "Slit her throat, huh? You know the reason `he did it?"

"Yes, but I'd just as soon not go into it. Now, will you please go after him, Depu...er, I mean, Marshal..." She scowled at him curiously. "What are we to call you now? Marshal *Rio Grande Kid*?"

"I don't know. The job's so fresh, I reckon I haven't studied on it." The man lumbered out from around his desk to grab his hat off a peg by the door and stand in the open doorway behind Julia, filling it. "Every time I glance down and see this five-pointed star on my vest, I get the shivers."

He stared into the street, his expression one of grave consternation. "Mister Hopkins, you say?" He ran a hand across his mouth and chin. "Him and several other fellas...a natty-lookin' crew of easterners, by the look of 'em...rode out of town about an hour ago. They was galloping like the devil's hounds were nipping at their heels."

"They were leaving town?" Julia asked, moving toward the big man in the doorway.

"Yep." Again, the flustered man scrubbed a hand across his mouth and chin. "Headed west as though they had somewhere to get to out there. Last night, after the train pulled in, several wagons left town. Big wagons. Ore drays. With a big work crew and a feller who looked like their foreman. Leastways, they must've been a work crew of some kind. They come in on the train—big, burly fellas."

"What on earth…?"

"That's what I thought. Oh, and another thing…" The new marshal of Apache Springs turned to Julia, his eyes round with incredulity. "Hopkins's gang was led out of town by more men who came in on the train last night."

"*More* men?"

"And these weren't just any men. There were a good half-dozen of 'em. Hardtails, every one. They was gunmen armed for bear!"

"You mean they were well-armed?"

"Yes, ma'am. That's what I mean, all right."

"Gunmen?"

"Hired guns, looked like to me. Hopkins and his pards must've hired 'em as guards." Again, the big man turned to stare out the door and to the east. "What could they be headin' for out there?" He moved his head a little. He must be looking at the stout express car Julia had spied on her way over to the jailhouse. "Must be they intend to move somethin' awful valuable in that big stout iron rail car, too. Somethin' in need of a whole passel of protection."

"Some kind of treasure," Julia said, stepping up beside

the Rio Grande Kid and following his gaze to the east.

"Yeah, treasure," the Kid said. "Most like." His tone thoughtful and more than a little dark, he added, "They must have discovered treasure out thataway...sure enough."

The thought obviously nettled him.

"Well, be that as it may, *Marshal*," Julia said, emphasizing the word to remind the man of his duties, "it doesn't change the fact that John Clare Hopkins murdered Candace Jo. He's a murderer, and you need to arrest..."

Julia let the words dwindle into silence.

The rataplan of fast hoofbeats sounded on her left. She turned her head to see a rider thundering in from the east. It was none other than her own sister, Emma, on her traditional sleek but now dusty and froth-silvered buckskin. Horse and rider skidded to a stop before the jailhouse and each woman yelled the other's name at the same time.

"What the hell are you doing here?" Emma asked as her dust caught up to her, touched with the buttery tones of the early light.

"I was about to ask you the same thing."

"Where's Yakima?"

"He rode out earlier to visit Pa."

"Ah, hell—I missed him, then!" Emma glanced over her shoulder. "I took a secondary trail...thought Pa might have me followed.

"Why would he—?"

"Never mind," Emma said, her own voice brittle and loud with emotion. "Where's John Clare Hopkins?"

Julia blinked, startled. "Why are *you* looking for him?"

"Cause he's up to no good, that's why!" Emma canted her head to study her older sister with a renewed, deeper curiosity than before, quickly flicking her gaze to the Rio Grande Kid standing beside her. "What's goin' on?"

"Hopkins killed one of my girls. Cut her throat."

Emma studied Julia, a wash of mismatched thoughts shunting around behind her pupils. "Where is he?"

"Left town," said the Rio Grande Kid, stepping out of the jail office and ambling on down the porch steps. "I was about to get after him."

"Good," Emma said. "I'll ride with you."

"No, you won't," the Kid said, heading in the direction of the livery barn. "This is official business an' you're just a kid!"

Emma turned her horse and nudged it in the same direction as the old marshal. "I'll meet you at the barn. I need a fresh hoss!"

"You listen to me, girl. I'm on official business, an' you're a mere citizen, so you stay outta my way—you hear me?"

"Shut up, old man!" Emma said, putting the buckskin into a gallop past the stout marshal, leaping the new rails and heading toward the mouth of a cross street. "We're gonna do this my way, and you'd best not trifle with me!"

"Trifle with *you*? Why, goddamnit, I just the other day taught a whole passel of Cheery-cowy Apaches how it's *me* you don't trifle with, little girl!" He waved his clenched fist at Emma, who just then disappeared around the corner of Senora Galvez's whorehouse.

Julia stared after them, crestfallen. One was young and crazy, the other old and feeble.

She wished Yakima was here.

21

Emma was also wishing Yakima was here.

As she canted her rented horse along beside the beefy old-timer who ludicrously called himself the Rio Grande Kid, she glanced at the man and had second thoughts about how much help he'd be when she finally confronted John Clare Hopkins and the men he'd apparently called in to plunder the ancient church. The so-called "Kid" must have been pushing seventy, but he'd have a hard time pushing anything but old age, as out of shape as he appeared.

Each of his thighs, clad in greasy buckskin, were larger around than Emma's waist. His belly sagged like a gunny sack full of piglets, pushing his checked wool shirt well out over his saddle horn as he rode. His face resembled the side of a falling down barn that had seen way too many hot suns, stiff winds, and cold winters.

Still, he was all Emma had. Not even she was foolhardy enough to face Hopkins's crew alone. She had a rifle in her saddle scabbard and a pistol in her saddlebags, but she'd need a whole lot more than that to even come close to evening the tall odds against her.

She needed someone to back her play, whatever that play would be. She'd learned all too well during her skirmish with the Bundrens how things turned out when she tried to go it alone.

As they kept their horses to canters, saving the horses for the several miles they'd have to ride, the old skudder and Emma's unlikely trail partner turned to her, scowling beneath the brim of his badly battered hat. "Where they headed, Miss Kosgrove? You know, don't you—or I've missed my guess."

The tracks of nearly a dozen horseback riders and three heavy wagons were plain in the desert caliche beneath the hooves of Emma's buckskin and the Kid's beefy sorrel splashed with white spots across its chest and withers.

"I think I do. I hope not, but I fear like hell I do."

"Where?"

Emma scowled as she studied the vast red desert bristling around them, toward the higher, forbidding bald crags of the heart of the Sierra Estrada, which, Emma feared, is where they were headed. For that's where the secret canyon lay.

She shook her head. "I can't tell you."

The old man's scowl deepened the maze of crevices in his puffy face. "What're you talkin' about? I'm gonna find out sooner or later, ain't I?"

"I just can't do it," Emma said, stubbornly clinging to the notion that she had to keep the canyon a secret at all costs.

"That's all right." The Kid turned his head back forward as they both nudged their mounts into lopes, chewing up more ground more quickly. "I think I know."

Emma turned quickly to him, her own frown intensifying. "You do?"

"Yes, I do. And I think it's all my fault, too. Dammit!" The Kid shook his head in disgust with himself.

Emma stared at him, incredulous. Was he just trying to trick her into telling him about the canyon, or did he already know? Studying him further while he rode about ten feet off her left stirrup, the wind basting the brim of his old Stetson against his forehead, she decided his claim was guileless.

The old man seemed a little too soft in the head for guile.

"Well?" she yelled above the thudding of their horses' hooves. "Are you going to tell me what in the hell you're talkin' about?"

He glanced at her quickly, nudged out of what appeared a sincere reverie. He slowed his mount to a trot, saving his horse for the longer ride ahead, and Emma did likewise, looking down once more to make sure they were still on Hopkins' trail. She edged the buckskin a little closer to her partner's sorrel, so she could hear his raspy voice above the clacking of their horse's shod hooves.

"I had a friend. His name was Eddie. This was in my old outlaw days, ya understand." The Kid cast Emma a smile of pride for days gone by, for the adventure he once had known. "Oh, I was a bad one in them days. Whang tough, an' make no mistake!" He slapped his thigh. "I was hell on the Texas border, an' that how they started callin' me the Rio—"

"Would you just get on with it?" Emma regaled the wool-gathering old-timer.

The Kid flushed with chagrin and brushed his sleeve across his nose. "Oh...right, right. As I was sayin', me an' Eddie split up on our way back up north from Baja. Our trail was hot. Boy, was it hot!" Immediately catching himself at the head of another digression, he said quickly, "Anyway...Eddie came up through this part of Arizona, trough the Sierra Estrada. I rode up through the Mojave Ridges. Eddie found an old church in a little canyon. Just stumbled on it by accident."

He turned to narrow a grave eye at Emma. "He said it was stuffed with more gold and a whole assortment of treasure in an old Spanish treasure box, plus an all-gold cannon, than him and me could ever imagine even if we put both our heads together on it for the next twenty years!"

"Well, I'll be damned," Emma muttered, staring in shock at the old man trotting his horse beside hers. Eddie must have stumbled on the canyon one of the rare times Jesus had left it, maybe to hunt or to fetch supplies from Nogales.

The Kid adjusted the set of his hat, staring straight ahead along the trail, squinting his eyes against the sun. "Eddie drew a map of the area where he found the treasure. He drew it on the back of an old wanted dodger announcing a bounty on himself." The old man chuckled and wagged his head. "That was Eddie for you. He'd show off that circular to the whores in—"

"So, you ended up with the map?"

The Kid cleared his throat, a little embarrassed by the whore talk. "Yeah. Not long after me an' Eddie rendezvoused in Phoenix, we was ambushed. Eddie died soon after, from his wounds, and he turned the map over to me. Before I ended up in the territorial pen, I buried the map. I dug it up after I was let out a few years ago for good behavior. That's what brought me to this country, ya see. I finally scraped up enough of a stake to come look for that canyon."

"So, where's the map?"

"I lost it! I couldn't make heads or tails of it anyway... and then I ran into ole Yakima an' he offered the deputy town marshal's job, an'—"

"How'd you lose it, you old fool?" Emma regaled the old blowhard, incensed that he might be the reason that canyon was about to be discovered, if it hadn't been already.

The Kid cast her a hurt look. "Now, don't go talkin' to me like that. I might have a nasty outlaw past, as bad as the worst, by god, but I got feelin's just like ever'body else!"

"How'd you lose the map?" Emma repeated—slowly, so even a moron could understand. Not that he was a moron, but he was old and he did seem a little feeble-minded, not to mention way too much in love with his so-called "outlaw" past. She had trouble picturing the man as much of a firebrand. But, then, she trusted hardly anyone even a few years older than she was, so she knew she probably wasn't giving the Rio Grande Kid a fair shake.

She didn't have time for fair shakes.

"I socked it away in the back of my Bible," the Kid told her, grimacing miserably. "I reckon it wasn't so much of a secret. Hell, Yakima knew about it. I had the Bible stowed away in the desk I shared with Galveston—you know, back in the office. I'd take it out and look at the map from time to time, just sort of worry it over in my head, wondering where that blasted 'X' could be, an' I reckon others seen me. Even prisoners we had locked up the jail cells."

He punched his thigh with his right fist. "You got it right, Miss Emma. I *am* a damn fool, an' make no mistake!"

Suddenly, Emma felt sorry for the oldster. She supposed getting old wasn't easy. The Kid was only trying to keep his self-respect, and some of the manhood he likely felt slipping away from him in the drift of years…

Still, the map.

"Who do you think might've gotten a hold of it?" Emma asked.

"Your guess is as good as mine, Miss. I got a feelin' it was some prisoner who stole it out of my Bible, after we let him out of his cell, an' maybe he sold it to Mister Hopkins."

He shook his head quickly. "Well, anyway…I wasn't gonna find that canyon even *with* the map. I couldn't make heads or tails out of it. I'm out here to bring Mister Hopkins back to town on murder charges."

"Right," Emma said, nodding. "Right…"

Maybe that would be enough to at least stall Hopkins' plundering of the church.

The Kid turned a curious look to her, his shaggy brows now coated in trail dust. "Say…why are you so bound and determined to run down Hopkins, anyways? In all the commotion over the dead doxie, I forgot to ask. Are you after that treasure yourself, Miss Emma?"

"No, I'm surely not."

Briefly, she told the oldster about old Jesus and the Apache witch's curse on the canyon. Or, more specifically, on anyone who tries to remove the treasure from the canyon. She also told about her vow to old Jesus about keeping would-be plunderers away from the church.

"Now," the Kid said, regarding the girl with awe. "That's a mighty tall order for one young gal—don't you think, Miss Emma?"

"Yes, I do. But do it I must."

"That's what you been spendin' your time doin' out here—makin' sure no one finds that church?"

Emma stared straight ahead. She did not reply. She knew how crazy it all sounded, and it made her feel a little foolish. But only a little.

"You got a life to live, Miss Emma," the Kid said, glancing at a rattlesnake that had crossed the trail ahead of them and then curled itself into a coil to the left of the trail—far enough away to be no real threat. When they'd passed the snake, he turned to Emma again. "You can't spend your whole life like ole Jesus, livin' in some ancient canyon, tryin' to protect some ancient treasure that may or may not be cursed."

"Oh, it's cursed, all right. Rusty Tull learned that the hard way."

"Rusty who...?"

"Never mind. I think you were off fetchin' that prisoner back from Tucson when the Bundrens showed up in Apache Springs." Emma shook her head in frustration. "Never mind, Mister Kid. You don't have to believe me. All you have to do is haul John Clare Hopkins back to Apache Springs on that murder charge. That'll give me time to think of another way to keep the treasure safe. If there is a way," she added under her breath, feeling her determination waning. Suddenly, what she'd promised Jesus she'd do seemed even more impossible than it had before.

She and the Kid rode for another hour, stopping their horses once to give them a blow and to water them. The Kid walked to the top of an outcropping to glass the country ahead of them. He walked back down, shaking his head and returning his field glasses to their case.

"No sign of 'em. When they left town this mornin', they were pushin' hard."

Emma rose from the rock she'd been sitting on while her horse had drawn water from her hat. "That means they've seen the canyon, all right. They know what's in there, an' they're not gonna waste any time gettin' the treasure out of that canyon and aboard that express car."

The thought made her feel like throwing up.

A half hour later, she led the Kid into the canyon

well-concealed by a rim of rocks and boulders strewn around its lip, so that you had to enter a forest of rock before following a winding, narrow path through even more rock as you dropped into the canyon itself. As she rode, Emma glanced uneasily over her shoulder, habitually wary of revealing the canyon to anyone, much less to a man who'd once been looking for it, hoping to get rich off what the church contained.

"You have to promise," she called behind her, their horses kicking up a good bit of red dust that wafted thickly amongst the devil's toothy mouth of rocks bristling around them, "that you won't tell anyone else about this."

Behind her the Kid wheezed a laugh, and spat dust from his lips. "I think the cat's been done let out of the bag, Miss Emma. Somehow, it looks like Hopkins found your treasure." He was gazing at the sloping ground beneath his sorrel's hooves. The tracks of the recent riders and wagons were as plain as the etchings on a china plate.

They told a horrible story of Emma's worst nightmare coming true.

They rode for another twenty minutes along the narrow canyon's rocky floor, following the arroyo's twisting, turning course to the east.

"Miss Emma?" the Kid said behind her, from where his sorrel followed close off the buckskin's tail.

"What is it?"

"If we're gettin' close, you let me take the lead, all right? I'll deal with Hopkins. The last thing either one of us needs is for you to go off half-cocked."

"Well," Emma said, squinting against the sunlight, staring ahead as the canyon's left wall fell back and the canyon opened up before her.

She jerked back on her buckskin's reins, and her heart leaped in her chest.

"Oh, my god!" she cried.

"Hold on, now, Miss Emma! Just hold on!"

Too late.

Emma ground her spurs into the buckskin's flanks and shot forward like a cannonball.

22

Del "T-Bone" Brown shifted the Henry rifle in his hands until the sights lined up on the chest of the big half-breed straddling a handsome black stallion. Brown was about to take up the slack in his trigger finger when the sun angled a bright ray down beneath the brim of his Stetson, momentarily blinding him.

"Go ahead," whispered his partner, Bry Thurmon, who crouched beside Brown, squeezing his own Winchester in his gloved hands.

Brown blinked, glanced away from the half-breed rider, then tried lining up the sights again. He shook his head and lowered the rifle, massaging his eyes still flaring from the assault of that bright ray with his thumb and index finger.

"What're you doin'?" Thurmon said in a raspy, scolding tone, scowling down at the big half-breed riding along the trail that hugged the base of the butte he and Brown were on. "Take the damn shot, Del!"

Brown shook his head as he watched the horse and rider just then disappear behind a thumb of the butte that bulged out over the trail, taking man and beast out of sight though Brown could hear the muffled thuds of the horse's hooves. "Sun's wrong."

"*What?* You had a clear shot at him!"

"I'll have a clearer one in a minute," Brown returned in an indignant tone, keeping his voice low. "And without the sun in my eyes."

He heaved himself up off his knees, swung to his left, and climbed a little farther up on the rocks strewn around the side of the bluff. When he gained a narrow shelf roughly fifteen feet up from where he'd just been, he dropped to a knee again and stared down the butte's north side, where the trail appeared again as it swung back from behind the jutting thumb.

Thurmon climbed up behind Brown and knelt to his left.

"See?" Brown said, giving his impatient partner a jeering grin. "Now I'll have a better shot—with no sun in my eyes. With this bastard, you wanna be certain-sure. I was told in Apache Springs he's tricky as hell."

"All right, all right. No sun. Just make that bullet count. Take him out clean so we can get the hell back to town."

"Hold on. Should be here in a second or two." Brown

lined up the Henry's sights on the spot on the trail he figured the half-breed would reappear as he and the horse clomped on around the far side of the bulging belly of the bluff.

Brown stared through the sights at the trail. He drew his index finger taut against the trigger, ready to squeeze as soon as horse and rider appeared again.

He waited. He could feel his heart beating in that finger drawn taut against the trigger. He stared down at the deserted trail.

"What the hell?" whispered Thurmon beside him.

The little heart in Brown's finger beat a little faster.

"Where is he?" Thurmon rasped in Brown's left ear.

Brown could hear the anxiety in his partner's voice. He could feel it in his own trigger finger. Still, he gazed through his sights at the trail on which at any second, he expected the big, half-breed former marshal of Apache Springs to reappear atop his handsome black stallion.

But horse and rider did not reappear. There was nothing down there but the slender horse trail littered with sand and gravel. Off the far side, a narrow canyon dropped.

When over a minute had passed, Brown lifted his gaze from his rifle sights. He turned to Thurmon, who was staring at him, frowning. Thurman asked in a soft, pinched voice that trembled slightly, "Where in the hell'd he go?"

Brown looked down the bluff to his right.

Nothing.

He looked behind him and Thurmon, along the bluff's shoulder.

Nothing.

He swung his head left to stare toward the bluff's crest. Still nothing.

His heart was racing now, kicking against the backside of his sternum. He was sweating, several beads rolling down his face.

"I don't like this," Thurmon said, his voice tight now as he whipped his gaze around wildly. "I don't like this at all. Where in the hell'd he go?"

"Here."

The quiet, mild voice had come from above. Quiet as it was, it was like a lightning bolt piercing Brown's chest. Both he and Thurmon jerked their wild-eyed gazes to the crest of the bluff.

"Oh," Thurmon said.

"Shit," said Brown.

The big half-breed stood on the bluff's crest, twenty or so feet straight above them. His long black hair buffeted behind his shoulders in the hot breeze rising from the canyon. His jade eyes smoldered with small hot fires of contained fury. His lips moved against his severely featured, copper-skinned face.

"You boys were gonna backshoot me."

Brown's heart skipped a couple of beats. He shared a fearful glance with Thurmon, whose open mouth formed a perfect 'O' against his long, angular face carpeted in several days' worth of brown beard stubble. The mole just off the corner of his right, gray eye twitched along with the vein beneath it.

Brown looked at the half-breed again. Henry's hands were empty. His single Colt .44 was still snugged down in the holster thonged on his right thigh clad in black broadcloth. He'd tucked the flap of his black frock coat back behind the staghorn grips, and he'd freed the keeper thong from over the hammer.

Brown squeezed the Henry rifle in his hands, wondering...

Could he raise the rifle, which was already cocked and ready to go, before the half-breed drew his Colt?

He cast a quick glance at Thurmon. The faint curl of a grin on Thurmon's lips told Brown that his partner was wondering the same thing and coming up with an optimistic answer.

Brown looked up at the half-breed.

The half-breed narrowed his eyes slightly, and quirked the corners of his broad mouth in a challenging smile.

Brown drew a deep breath, let it out. He squeezed the Henry in his hands. His heart was a wild stallion kicking and bucking inside him.

He jerked the rifle up, slamming the rear stock against his shoulder, and heard himself scream when he saw that he'd made a big mistake in underestimating the half-breed's speed. As he began to squeeze the Henry's trigger, the Colt in the half-breed's own gloved hand bucked and roared, blossoming red flames and pale smoke.

***

Yakima slid his Colt slightly right and squeezed the trigger once more, the second roar following so closely on the first one that both shots together sounded like a single shotgun blast.

Both of his stalkers flew screaming down the face of the bluff, their black suitcoats flapping like wings. Dust flew up around them.

One piled up with a smacking thud against a large rock protruding from the side of the bluff. The second one, the first man he'd shot, continued rolling down the bluff before landing with a thud onto the trail below.

Yakima leaped forward and descended the steep slope sideways, sort of leap-sliding to keep his feet. He paused over the man who'd piled up against the rock. The man's gray eyes stared up at him, opaque with death. Yakima's bullet had taken him through his low middle chest.

Yakima continued down the bluff, leaping onto the trail.

The second man lay writhing and pressing both his hands to his upper right side. His dusty face was a mask of agony. His long, thin, sandy brown hair flew about his oval-shaped face with a thin mustache that drooped down both sides of his mouth. He had a star-shaped scar on the nub of his chin.

Yakima stepped forward to straddle the man's writhing body, one of his boots off the man's right hip, the other off his left hip. He glared down at him.

"Who you ridin' for?"

The man glared up at him, his eyes bright with pain. He winced, his cheeks rising like two billiard balls, then grunted, "Go to hell."

"Might as well tell me. You'll be dead in three jangles of a whore's bell."

The man stared up at him, vaguely, fleetingly thoughtful behind the pain.

"Kosgrove? Or..." Yakima asked.

"Hopkins." The man shook his head slightly.

"Why?"

"Two reasons. The gold and Kosgrove's daughter."

Yakima frowned. "The gold?"

"The gold in the canyon."

Yakima continued frowning down at the man. He looked familiar. "You were with Booth. You an' Booth killed the Bundrens."

254

The dying man winced, writhed, kicking his right boot out with a pain spasm. "Hopkins and his brother hired us and several others to make sure no one found the gold before they could get to it."

Yakima spat to one side in anger. "There's enough gold in that church to make a dozen men richer than their wildest dreams."

"You damn fool," the dying man spat out. "Hopkins's greedier'n those twelve men put together."

"You were a fool to ride for that bastard. To try to *backshoot* me, you coward."

"Yeah, well, the joke's on you, you half-breed son of a bitch!" The dying man was dying fast. He'd barely gotten those words out, hissing and snarling like a leg-trapped bobcat.

"What're you talkin' about?"

The dying man gave a crooked smile. "We left you a little surprise…in your room…in Apache Springs."

Yakima's scowl deepened. "What kind of surprise?"

The dying man strangled on a laugh. "Go to hell…"

His eyes rolled back in his head, his head fell back on the trail and quivered a little as he died.

The man's last words echoed around inside Yakima's brain.

He holstered his Colt and ran back down the trail to where he'd left Wolf.

***

He galloped into Apache Springs a half-hour later.

Wolf leaped the twin rails splitting the main street in half and pulled up in front of the Conquistador Inn. This time of the day, there were few people out on the hotel's broad, sun-washed front veranda. One of those people, however, was Julia. She'd been pacing back and forth when Yakima had ridden up, but now she swung toward him, holding a mug of coffee in both her hands.

"Yakima!"

He tossed his reins over the hitchrail and stopped, gazing up at her through the dust wafting around him in the sparkling midday air.

She hurried along the veranda to stand atop the steps. "Hopkins!" She gritted her teeth, her eyes on fire. "He killed Candace Jo. Slit her throat!"

"Where'd you find her?"

"In his room. He told me she'd be there. He killed her because he...he knew...about us...last night." Her eyes turned sheepish. She opened and closed her hands around her coffee mug.

Yakima paused to think through the information. The Hopkins ambusher had told Yakima he'd find the surprise in his own room.

Yakima looked at Julia again. "Have you seen Rusty

Tull today?"

Julia frowned. "No. As a matter of fact, I forgot all about..."

She let the sentence die on her lips as Yakima hurried up the porch steps. Apprehension blazed inside him. As he reached the veranda, Julia looked up at him, walking along beside him as he entered the hotel. "Hopkins rode out of town earlier. With several men, including his brother Ferrell. Business associates and hired guns."

Yakima stopped and turned to her, incredulity furling his brows. "Why?"

"They're after something out there. Something valuable. They took three big wagons," she called as Yakima continued walking along the bar to the broad staircase at the rear. "Emma and your deputy rode out after them."

Again, Yakima stopped and turned back to her.

Christ, what the hell was going on? Why did he have the uneasy feeling a very large powder keg had exploded, and he'd been the last to know?

First things first. He had to get up to his room to check on Rusty.

"I'll be back in a minute," he said, then hurried up the stairs, one hand on the rail and taking two steps at a time.

He jogged along the second-floor hall to his room.

He twisted the knob. Unlocked. He shoved the door wide, took one step into the room, shuttling his gaze from left to right, and stopped cold in his tracks.

"You sons of bitches," he said slowly, under his breath, his heart striking his breastbone like a smithy's hammer.

Rusty Tull's slender body hung from a ceiling beam between the end of Yakima's bed and the wooden dresser abutting the room's right wall. The lanky redhead was clad only in his longhandles. His pale feet were bare. His stringy hair hid his eyes and part of his mouth.

His executioners—the two men now lying dead on Yakima's backtrail—must have found him in bed earlier this morning. They'd pulled him out of bed, tied a stout noose around his neck, and hoisted him up until the back of his head was snug against the ceiling beam.

They'd tied off the end of the rope to a leg of the heavy dresser, which had slid out a little from the wall, at an angle. The kid had fought them, of course. A picture had been knocked from the wall.

They'd choked off his screams with a dirty sock. The sock was still in the poor kid's mouth, slithering out of it like an oversized worm, the patched toe hanging down near the boy's skinny, floury white chest.

"Oh, my *god!*"

Yakima had been so shocked and enraged to find Rusty hanging dead from the beam that he'd only vaguely heard running footsteps in the hall outside his room. Now he turned to see Julia standing behind him, gazing up in horror at the poor dead redhead, one hand cupped to her mouth.

"They headed southwest, I take it," Yakima said and hurried back out of the room.

23

"*Fools!*" Emma screamed as she galloped toward the
church. "You damn *fools!*"

Gunshots ripped through the canyon, echoing like
thunder. Several bullets screeched through the air near
Emma and the buckskin.

A man shouted, "Trouble, Mister Hopkins!"

More gunfire, smoke puffing from the maws of rifles
facing Emma from in front of the church.

Emma drew back sharply on the buckskin's reins. The
horse skidded to a halt, Emma throwing up her empty
hands and screaming, "Hold your fire! Hold your fire!"
Her carbine was still in its scabbard, her pistol still in her
saddlebags. She knew she couldn't win a shoot-out with
these men. She wanted to talk reason to them, if possible.

She stared at the men before her. There were at least a
dozen forming a semi-circle out front of the church and

a large cream tent that had been set up in front of it and to its right side, near a small clump of mesquites.

Just now standing outside the tent and smoking a fat cigar was John Clare Hopkins and a shorter, younger man whom Emma knew to be the man's brother. Three other men, as well-groomed and as well-dressed in flashy suits as the Hopkins brothers, were just now stepping out of the tent, looking wary, tentative. They were also smoking cigars. One also held a shot glass in his hand. Another held a stout brown beer bottle.

Three wagons had been pulled up in front of the church. At least a dozen more men—large, beefy, bearded types who appeared day laborers or possibly miners—stood around the church, many of them wielding sledge hammers. They'd been slamming the hammers against the church walls, shattering the ancient adobe to get to the gold that lined the church's inside walls. Some now stood around the front door, having stepped out from the church's bowels to see what all the shooting had been about.

Emma held her reins taut in her gloved hands, facing the duster-clad, cold-eyed men Hopkins and his moneyed partners had apparently hired as guards and who now stood aiming rifles at her. A couple of these professional killers were down on one knee, staring with chilling flintiness at her through the sights of their Winchesters, daring Emma to come one more step closer.

One of them, a man with a thick, blond, soup-strain-er mustache and close-set eyes beneath the brim of his tobacco-brown Stetson, glanced over his shoulder at the well-dressed men standing in front of the tent. "It's a girl, Mister Hopkins. I'll kill her if you say so."

The man's threat was flatly indifferent. He might have been saying he was about to head to the grocery store for a pound of beef and a basket of eggs.

"Hold on." Hopkins glanced at his nattily dressed part-ners then walked forward, scowling. He stepped between two of the gunmen then shuttled his glance toward Emma to the workers standing around before the church. "What the hell are you men gawking at? I'm not paying you to stand around. Get to work!"

A couple of the workers resumed smashing their stout-headed hammers against the adobe walls.

"No!" Emma screamed, kicking the buckskin forward then drawing back on the reins again when one of the riflemen fired a warning shot perilously close to her head.

She jerked her head back, hair flying around her shoulders, then cast her horrified gaze to Hopkins. "You don't understand what you're doing! You can't do this! You can't take any of that treasure!"

"I can't, can I?" Hopkins said with a defiant, mocking grin. He tapped ashes from the end of his cigar and said, "Well, have a look." He gestured at the church. "That's exactly what I and my partners are doing."

Emma gaped in horror as the burly workers continued hammering at the church's walls, smashing large holes in the adobe. Gold plates flashed within those holes, some of the inside gold tiles tumbling onto the ground outside the church, along with the crushed adobe. As dull and dusty and sooty as it was, the sunlight still glistened off of it.

Two men emerged single-file from the church's doorless opening. They were hugging gold and silver candleholders and silver, jewel-encrusted chalices to their chests. They tramped over to one of the wagons and dumped the loot into straw-lined crates.

Jerking her gaze back to Hopkins, Emma said, "It's cursed! It's all cursed, you fool! You can't remove any of that treasure from this canyon!"

Hopkins stood before Emma, the grave-eyed gunman flanking him, still aiming their rifles at the girl. "What are you talking about, Emma? Cursed? What's cursed?"

Emma gestured with her left gloved hand. "The church! The treasure! All of it. An Apache witch cursed it after the earthquake that killed her people. They were enslaved by the Jesuits. They died mining that gold for the Jesuit priests. They died in the mines, in vain, all of them wiped out. The witch placed a hex on all of that gold...all of the treasure...so that if the fruits of her people's labor was ever exploited for personal gain..."

She let her words fade when Hopkins only laughed at her, glancing over his shoulder at his well-dressed partners walking up behind him, smoking and sipping. "Did you hear that, gentleman? The treasure is cursed? An old Apache witch placed a hex on it!"

"I don't put much stock in curses," said one of his partners, a small, dapper man with a very thin mustache and thick, bushy side whiskers. A silver-framed manacle dangled from the lapel of his dark-green frock coat. "But I've observed that you know some very beautiful women, John. I'll give you that, you old rascal!"

The man's eyes were fairly burning holes in Emma's dusty shirt.

"Where've you been hiding this one, John?" asked one of the others, poking a cigar between his thickly mustached, bright pink lips. He wore a long, broadcloth duster and wore a red silk sash around his potbellied waist. "She'd be a real corker...with a bath."

Ignoring the goatish fool, Emma turned back to Hopkins. "How did you find it? Was it the Kid's map? The treasure map from his Bible?"

Hopkins scowled uncertainly, furling his trimmed brows. "I don't know what you're talking about. More of your nonsense. For years, I've had professional investigators perusing the Jesuit mining archives in Mexico City. One of them found the plat for the old gold mine in this canyon, and sent it to me. This canyon, this church, is why I came to Apache Springs. I've been making arrangements with my brother and our associates"—he glanced at the men standing behind him—"to appropriate the gold and jewels in the church for months now. There are no laws against it. The treasure has been here for over a hundred years, for anyone's taking, including ours. Everything came together when the railroad reached Apache Springs and I had a way to ship the treasure to buyers back East." He shrugged. "It's a simple as that."

"You've been out here before today."

"Of course. I led a small, preliminary, investigatory contingent. We were careful to cover our tracks to makes sure no one followed us down here."

Which is exactly what Emma had done, so no one had followed her down here, either. But all of her efforts had been in vain. Hopkins had a map.

He glowered at her again, holding his cigar by his chin. "How did you find out about the treasure?"

"Never mind about that. It's not as simple as you think, Hopkins," Emma said, nearly cross-eyed with frustration. "I know it's hard for you to believe. But you'd better believe it. That treasure is cursed. You have to take your men and leave here now!"

"Leave all that gold?" laughed Hopkins's brother, whom Emma had never been formally introduced to but whose name she believed was Ferrell or something like it. "Why, you must be crazy!" He narrowed his hazel eyes skeptically. "How long have you known about this church, young lady?"

"For several years." Emma glanced once more in horror at the burly men smashing the adobe walls with reckless abandon while others plundered the church's innards for the treasure heaped atop the altar.

"And you've never taken a thing out of it?" asked Ferrell Hopkins, narrowing a disbelieving eye at her.

"No, I never have. I wouldn't. Not knowing what I know about it."

John Clare Hopkins himself said, "Well, what you know about it is going to have remain a secret. At least until we've finished plundering it." He glanced at the gunman who'd spoken before. "Grab her. Tie her up!"

"You killed the Bundrens to keep them quiet!" Emma coldly accused him, pointing a finger at the dapper Brit. "You *tried* to kill me and Yakima! You killed one of Julia's whores in the Conquistador. You're a cold-blooded killer, John Clare!"

"For chrissakes, grab her!" Hopkins shouted with exasperation at the guard.

"Don't you dare touch me!" Emma screamed.

The gunman lowered his rifle and lunged at Emma.

Emma kicked him in the chest and tried to turn her

horse. One of the other gunmen grabbed the buckskin's bridle strap, laughing and ogling the pretty girl. The first gunman cursed angrily, grabbed Emma's arm, and jerked her violently out of the saddle.

Emma screamed and hit the ground with a thud and a shrill cry, the wind knocked out of her.

Hopkins walked up to her. He'd drawn a pepperbox revolver from a shoulder holster inside his frock coat. Now he stood over Emma, raised the stubby pistol, and clicked the hammer back. He narrowed one eye as he aimed down at Emma's head. "I do apologize, my dear. But I'm afraid you've—"

"Hold it!"

Sitting up, her head spinning from the fall, Emma glanced around her horse, which had turned full around during the melee, and saw the Rio Grande Kid walk up out of the brush, cacti, and rocks that littered the arroyo that ran down the middle of the canyon. The stout old man held a double-barrel shotgun straight out from his right shoulder. He narrowed one eye as he stared down the large double bores at John Clare Hopkins.

He clicked both heavy hammers back with solid, ratcheting clicks.

"Get away from her, you infernal horse's ass, or I'll shred that hundred-dollar suit with you in it!"

Hopkins had whipped his startled eyes to the so-called Kid, who had little Kid left in him. No, that wasn't true, Emma saw now. She thought she glimpsed in his eyes the glitter of a much younger man, a young fire-brand who still felt the thrill of throwing caution to the wind and playing out a hand even when the odds were stacked against him.

"You fat old dog!" Hopkins barked. "How dare you confront me like this! Are you too stupid to not only have no respect for your betters but to not know when you are *severely outgunned?*"

The Kid stopped about ten feet away from Hopkins and the gunmen flanking him, their rifles now trained on the old man himself. The Kid kept his hard, defiant gaze on John Clare, wrinkling his broad nose with disdain. "You can put a hat on a mule, but that don't make him a man. If these gun rats of yours don't lower their weapons, I'm gonna blow a hole through you big enough to drive the Southern Pacific through. On the count of three!"

He squeezed the shotgun in his hands as he aimed at Hopkins belly and drew his index finger taut against one of the Greener's triggers.

"Lower your weapons!" Hopkins shouted, throwing a hand up to emphasize the order. "Lower them now!" When a couple of the gunman, not used to giving quarter, especially to old men, were slow to lower their Winchesters, Hopkins barked hoarsely and more loudly,

"*Lower them now, for chrissakes! Did you hear what I said? He* means *it!*"

The men quickly albeit reluctantly lowered their rifles.

Glancing at Emma, the Kid said, "On your feet, girl. Climb atop your horse an' split the wind outta here."

Wincing against the pain in her head and in her hip, which took the brunt of the hard tumble, Emma gained a knee and then her feet. She'd lost her hat, and now she swept her flaxen hair out of her eyes. "Where's your horse, Kid?"

Talking to Emma but keeping his hard gaze on Hopkins, the Kid said, "Up the trail apiece. I'll be along shortly."

Emma walked up to her horse, keeping her own worried eyes on the Kid. "You won't make it."

"I ain't that old. Hop aboard!"

"I mean they'll close in on you before you can make it to your horse, Kid. As soon as you're out of range with your Greener, they'll cut you down with their rifles."

"Hop aboard, dammit, girl!"

Emma leaped up onto the buckskin's back. She looked at Hopkins and the gunmen. They stood with their guns lowered, but they regarded the Rio Grande Kid with shrewd, savage curls to their mouths and wolfish glitters in their eyes. Emma whipped the horse around to face the Kid.

269

She patted the buckskin's rump. "Come on, Kid! Hop aboard! We'll ride double!"

The Kid, keeping his Greener aimed at Hopkins's belly, shook his head. "I gotta keep this gut-shredder aimed at this overdressed magpie here, or they'll cut us both down for sure."

"You're smarter than you look," said the mustached rifleman with a leering grin.

"Ride out, Emma!"

"No!"

"Goddammit!" The Kid was red-faced mad.

That changed her mind. If she didn't do what he'd told her to do, what he'd just done to save her life would be in vain.

"*All right!*" she screamed then neck-reined the buckskin back around and ground her spurs into its flanks. She let out a strangled sob. "Goddamnit, Kid!"

***

The Kid turned his entire body partly, so he could keep the girl and the buckskin in the corner of his left eye while maintaining his focus, as well as the twelve-gauge shotgun, on John Clare Hopkins's belly.

"I'll be seein' you later," the Kid told Hopkins, "about the murder of Candace Jo at the Conquistador."

The younger Hopkins turned to his brother, frowning. "Candace Jo...?"

"Soiled dove," the Kid said. "Your brother cut her throat from ear to ear."

Ferrell Hopkins's scowl grew more intense. The rest of Hopkins's moneyed partners looked at John Clare, as well.

"Oh, you didn't know your brother was a cold-blood killer," the Kid told the younger brother.

John Clare smiled smugly at the lawman. "He's lying, I assure all of you. I would never do such a thing—especially to such a pretty young woman. And one with so many talents."

"Yeah, well, like I said," the Kid said, starting to back away in the direction Emma had gone, "I'll be talkin' to you about that later."

Hopkins's oily, arrogant smile broadened. "Oh, I don't think there's going to be any later for you, old man." He slid his glance to the nearly dozen gimlet-eyed gunmen holding their rifles down low by their sides. None said anything, but the Kid could tell they'd gotten the message.

As soon as he'd taken a few more steps up the trail, and his Greener was out of effective range, they were to go to work with the Winchesters and Henrys. The thought formed a lump at the far south end of the Kid's throat.

He'd gotten himself into a good one, hadn't he? Well,

he'd been bound to sooner or later. Besides, there was no point in growing much older. What did he have to look forward to? He'd had a good long life. Old men on the frontier weren't treated much better than old, useless dogs.

He'd had a good run—the high points being his defeat of the Chiricahuas who'd attacked the stage and when Yakima Henry had shown enough confidence in him to pin the five-pointed, silver-washed star on his vest. He might have been a windy old bag of suet and several other unfortunate things, but at least he had those notches on the proverbial gun handle.

He continued walking backward, keeping the heavy Greener aimed at Hopkins and the others. As Hopkins and his business partners slowly shuffled back behind the rifle-wielding hardcases, all of whom had their stony eyes riveted on the Kid, that lump in the Kid's throat grew a tad larger and tighter.

One more step, his spurs chinging.

Two more steps.

Three...

Standing behind the riflemen, Hopkins smiled at the Kid, and winked. "Sleep tight, you old scoundrel. Don't let the diamondbacks bite!"

All at once, the riflemen raised their Winchesters and Henrys, loudly pumping cartridges into the rifles' actions and pressing the rear stocks against their shoulders. Hopkins raised his arm, as though he were about to flag the start of a horserace, then whipped that arm down, shouting, "Kill the old fool!"

A rifle thundered, causing the Kid to give a violent start.

He hesitated, then continued shuffling backward, frowning at the gunmen. But he saw no smoke nor any other indication that any of them had fired his rifle. What he did see was John Clare's head snap back, as though he'd been punched. When the dapper Englishman's head wobbled forward again, the Kid saw a dark round spot in the man's pale forehead about the size of a silver dollar.

John Clare's eyes crossed then rolled back in his head as his head tipped back again. His knees buckled, and he piled up on the ground like the empty suit he'd always been.

The men around the man turned to him in shock.

The Kid swung his own head to look behind him, up the trail that ran along the base of the canyon's high north wall. A black-hatted man was on one knee atop a low outcropping about forty yards behind the kid, near the canyon wall. Now Yakima Henry cupped a hand to his mouth and shouted, "Turn around an' run, Kid. Run like you was twenty again. I'll try to hold them off, but no guarantees!"

The Kid's old ticker kicked in his chest.

"Oh, boy. Oh, boy!"

He swung around, stumbling over his own clumsy feet. He dropped to a knee, scrambled to his feet again, and began lumbering up the trail, icy spiders of dread crawling up and down his back when he heard Ferrell Hopkins scream behind him, "Kill them! *Goddamnit, kill them all!*"

24

Careful to aim over the Rio Grande Kid running toward him, Yakima cut loose on Hopkins's hired guns. He was perched atop an escarpment of broken boulders, and the Kid was running toward him, below him on his right, following the trail that hugged the north side of the canyon.

Yakima was a little too far away for deadly shooting, and a good bit of chaparral bristled between him and the church and the cream tent out front of it, but as he triggered and pumped the Yellowboy, the rifle roaring and leaping in his hands, he watched at least three of the riflemen go down, clutching wounds.

He popped his last cap and sent the empty cartridge hurling over his right shoulder to clatter onto the rocks behind him. As he did, he saw several of the gunmen running into the brush flanking the tent. Ferrell Hopkins was lying belly down on the ground, where he'd dropped with his silver-spooned cohorts, taking cover, his arms crossed on his head as though to shield himself from one of Yakima's .44 rounds.

"Get mounted and get after him! I don't want that shooter or anyone else leaving this canyon alive! God *damn* that man—whoever he is!"

Yakima looked at the Yellowboy. He'd lowered the cocking lever, and now he stared into the open action. Smoke slithered around inside the breech, smelling like rotten eggs. He started to pinch cartridges from his cartridge belt, intending to reload and resume shooting, but reconsidered.

He was outnumbered. Even with the high ground, he didn't have a chance against those shooters, there being at least nine left. They'd surround the escarpment and pick him off like shooting a turkey out of a tree. Besides, he had to get the Kid and Emma clear of the killers.

That thought foremost in his mind, he scrambled to his feet and hurried down the backside of the escarpment. A few of the riflemen were triggering lead toward him. The bullets screamed off rocks as Yakima leaped off a boulder and onto the ground beside the coyote dun gelding he'd rented at Gramps Dawson's Livery & Feed Barn. Wolf had been spent from the long ride back to town from Kosgrove.

He jumped onto the horse's back, startling the mount,

who was no more accustomed to him than Yakima was the horse. At such a time, he wished he had trusty, stalwart Wolf, but it was just him and the rental horse, so, hoping for the best, he put spurs to the gelding's flanks and crouched forward.

The horse gave an indignant whinny as it lunged off its rear hooves and lunged headfirst into a hard run. Yakima could feel the horse's back muscles twitching nervously beneath the saddle as the bullets Hopkins's gunslicks were firing clattered off the rocks and plunked into the ground around the trail.

"I bet you're wishin' it would have been anyone but me that came lookin' for a horse today—eh, boy?" Yakima said as he and the horse shot up the trail. "I wouldn't blame you a bit!"

As he and the coyote dun followed a bend in the canyon wall, Yakima saw the Kid down on both knees just ahead.

"Whoah, hoss!" Yakima jerked back on the dun's reins.

As the horse skidded to a stop beside the Kid, the older man looked up at Yakima, red-faced, shaking his head with exhaustion. "I'm spent! You go on ahead!"

"It's only a little ways to your horse, Kid!" He couldn't see the Kid's sorrel from here, but he knew the Kid had tied it only sixty or so yards down canyon, having wanted to steel up on the pillagers in silence. Yakima flung out his left hand. "Hop on board!"

"Ah, hell, you'll make better time without this damn rain barrel behind you!"

Guns were popping and hooves were thundering behind Yakima, who snapped his hand at the Kid and said, "I'm not going anywhere without you, Kid, so the sooner you take my hand and crawl aboard this rented cayuse, the better off we'll both be!"

The Kid snapped a wide-eyed glance behind him. The first few riders were caroming into view, dusters winging out behind them, savage fury glinting in their eyes. A couple of Hopkins's rannies triggered carbines, and the bullets sliced the air around Yakima and the Kid, who cursed, heaved himself to his feet, and shoved his hand at Yakima.

Yakima closed his hand around the Kid's. He'd sidled the dun over to a rock, so the big man had a relatively easy time hopping aboard. When the Kid had settled his weight behind Yakima, Yakima nudged the dun's flanks with his spurs and bellowed, "Go, hoss—go *now*!"

The horse glanced back at him, its eyes wide and white-ringed with anxiety, not caring one bit for the bullets screeching around him and sawing into the chaparral. It turned its head forward, laid back its ears, and bolted up the trail with less speed than before, which was understandable, since the Kid added well over two hundred pounds.

The canyon floor slanted upward.

Bullets curled the air around Yakima and the Kid, the older man waving at one as though at a pesky fly. "That was so close I won't need to shave that side tomorrow… if there *is* a tomorrow!"

Yakima didn't have to look behind to know that the gunslicks were closing on them fast. The thunder of their horses was getting quickly louder, as was the belching of their rifles. Fortunately, as the coyote dun turned to the right, around a bend in the canyon wall, Yakima saw the Kid's sorrel standing just ahead, its ears pricked and its tail arched.

"Quick, Kid!" Yakima yelled. "I'll cover you!"

He was about to rip his .44 from its holster but stopped when a voice to his right said, "Keep riding, boys! I'll cover you both!"

Yakima looked over to see Emma step out from the base of the canyon wall. She had her buckskin's ribbons in one hand, her Winchester carbine in the other. She dropped to a knee and aimed her rifle toward where the gunslicks would be tearing around the bend in the canyon wall in about three seconds.

"I thought I told you to stay on the ridge!" Yakima yelled.

Emma pumped a cartridge into her Winchester's action. "I don't take orders from any man!" As the Kid struggled up onto his sorrel's back, Emma smiled over her shoulder at Yakima. "They take orders from *me*!"

Just then, the first wave of Hopkins's riders came thundering around a bend in the trail. Emma went to work with her carbine, aiming quickly and shooting. Two riders flew out of their saddles while another sagged back and sideways, blood geysering from the wound in his chest. He dragged his horse to the ground where the screaming mount lay on top of him, flailing.

Another rider rode up behind the fallen horse and rider, and that horse tripped over the fallen one, and a second later there were two down horses and one down man, raging and screaming. Dust rose thickly.

Yakima unsheathed his Colt and swung down from the dun's back. He fired into the roiling cloud of dust, holding the rest of the riders back behind the bulge in the canyon wall.

He glanced at Emma. "Get on your horse and hightail it to the top of the ridge!"

"No!" Emma pumped another cartridge into her Winchester's action and strode toward the roiling dust cloud. "We have to kill them all!"

Yakima felt an odd shuddering beneath his boots. He glanced across the canyon, to his right, and saw several boulders tumbling down the ridge wall.

Holy shit...

Yakima shoved his Colt back into its holster. He

grabbed Emma by the back of her neck and the seat of her pants, and threw her up onto the buckskin's back.

"This is one man you take orders from today, young lady!"

"Goddamn you!" she screamed, barely holding onto her Winchester.

Yakima jerked the buckskin around and slammed his Colt against its left hip. Horse and rider shot up the trail. By now the Kid was mounted. Yakima hooked his thumb at him, indicating up trail.

"Hightail it, Kid," he shouted. "I'm right behind you!"

"You don't have to tell me twice! *Hi-yahhh!*" The Kid jammed steel to the sorrel's flanks, hunkered low over the horse's mane and barreled up the trail.

Yakima looked toward the bulge in the canyon wall. At the same time, one of Hopkins's men snaked a rifle around the bend, aiming at Yakima. Yakima triggered a shot at him. The man cursed and pulled his rifle back behind the bulge.

Spying movement to his right, Yakima turned to see two more boulders tumbling down the canyon's south wall, bouncing off the ridge and loosing more boulders in their wake. A loud rumbling grew louder as the rockslide grew in size.

Beneath his boots the ground shook, and more, even louder rumbling reached his ears. He looked up and his blood froze when he saw a cabin-sized boulder hurling down from the bridge nearly directly above him. He was holding onto the coyote dun's reins, and the horse screamed and pitched when it heard the roar that was like that of an oncoming locomotive. Yakima felt the wind-whip of the boulders' passing, and watched it arc out from the canyon wall and plunge into the boulder and cactus-filled arroyo now on his left as he peered up trail.

A deafening thunder rattled his eardrums and caused the ground to quake beneath his boots as the boulder crashed and bounced and tumbled toward the narrow canyon's far ridge. Dust roiled thickly, shroud-like, and the air smelled like the inside of a grave.

More roaring sounded and the ground continued to pitch and shudder as Yakima hurled himself onto the dun's back. He slapped his reins against the horrified mount's left hip, and, screaming, the horse ran up the trail as though its tail were on fire.

Yakima didn't look up toward the ridge crest. At least, not directly. In the upper periphery of his vision he could see more and more boulders come crashing down from the canyon's lip two hundred feet above him. He heard the tooth-splintering cacophony of the large rocks plunging into the arroyo around him. A shadow arced over him, as quick as a blink, and the crashing roar of the boulder striking the canyon just beyond him, on his left, nearly knocked him out of his saddle.

The dun jerked with a start and lifted its head and gave another terrified whinny, fighting the bit.

Yakima kept his head down and his spurs rammed up taut against the dun's flanks. If it wavered or slowed in the slightest, took the slightest misstep and fell, horse and rider were doomed. They were probably doomed anyway, for Yakima could see and hear the canyon fairly collapsing around him, but the coyote dun's speed was his only chance to make it to the lip of the canyon without being smashed like a bug with a hammer.

Amidst the roar of boulders behind him and to his left, as more and more rocks plunged down his side of the canyon, Yakima heard the muffled wails and screams of Hopkins's men caught in the stony torrent. He heard the screaming of the dying men's horses.

Around him, rock dust billowed like that of a raging sandstorm. For maybe a hundred or two hundred yards of hard riding, horse and rider rising slowly with the trail hugging the canyon's north wall, he could barely see ten feet ahead of him.

He covered his mouth and nose with his arm. It was hard to judge how long he'd been in the saddle, how far he'd ridden away from the church, for all of his senses were oddly scrambled and muted. He couldn't have been more disoriented had he been in a stagecoach that had caromed off a perilous trail to roll and bang its way down a long steep ridge toward a gorge.

He and the dun managed to get out ahead of the billowing dust. Instinctively, the horse followed the trail to the right, where the trace sloped up gently toward the ridge on this far northwestern, and shallower, end of the canyon.

The deep, ominous rumbling continued behind Yakima.

The dun slowed a little as it approached the crest of the ridge, coming up through the chaparral and widely scattered rocks, near where Emma had encountered the Bundrens and Rusty Tull. He saw her now, sitting her horse just down from the ridge's lip, staring toward him, concern on her brow and in her almond-shaped, hazel eyes. She was as dusty as any Texas-to-Kansas trail rider, and her hair hung in wild tangles. She still held her carbine down against her thigh.

"Yakima!"

She waved the rifle.

The Rio Grande Kid sat his tired, sweat-silvered, dust-coated sorrel beyond her, on the ridge's crest. He was staring out over the canyon, his eyes wide, lips moving as he muttered softly to himself, incredulously.

Yakima put the dun up past Emma and clomped onto the rocky ridge crest. He swung the tired dun back to the east, climbing the rock-strewn slope near the canyon's cut. A great cloud of dust billowed to the southeast, in the direction of the church.

The roaring still sounded, but not as loudly as before. He could still feel the rumbling in the ground beneath the dun's hooves, as though the stirrings of some giant buried beast.

Yakima swung heavily out of the saddle. He sleeved dust that had caked around his eyes and walked a little farther up the rise, staring back along the ridge to the east. There'd once been a devil's playground of boulders there, capping the ridge and obscuring the mysterious arroyo. Now, the ground was open, for all of that rock had tumbled, as though pushed from the ridge crest by an angry god's giant arm, into the canyon itself.

The canyon was no more. Now it was a giant boulder field that reached almost to the level desert on which Yakima now stood, staring with his lower jaw hanging in shock and exasperation. The canyon and the church and all of that treasure was sealed up in a billion-ton sarcophagus.

Along with the men who'd come to pillage it.

Footsteps sounded behind him. Emma stepped up beside him, on his right, and cast her gaze out over the canyon—over what *had been* the canyon only minutes before. More footsteps sounded, spurs sang softly. The Rio Grande Kid shuffled heavily, wearily up on Yakima's left. He spat to one side.

The older man stared off over the former canyon that was now just a giant boulder field obscured by an even larger, mushroom-shaped cloud of rock dust. The dusk obscured the sun, so that all three weary riders found themselves in an eerie, artificial twilight world of shadows and dust.

Emma glanced at Yakima, narrowing one eye. "You believe me now? About the witch?"

Yakima hiked a shoulder and continued to stare out over the giant boulder field now hiding forever the *Arroyo de la Muerte*, the Canyon of Death.

"Believe in her or not," the Kid said with a long, weary sigh. "She sure knows how to skin a cat—don't she?"

He spat more dust from his lips and wheezed a tired laugh.

Epilogue

That night, after a long soak in a hot tub and a thick steak with a platter of potatoes, Yakima crawled into his bed at the Conquistador Inn. He'd locked his door and wedged a chair under it to keep out possible callers.

Callers were unwanted tonight. He intended to hit the trail early, and he needed a good night's sleep. He hadn't had a sound night's shut-eye in a month of Sundays. In fact, he wasn't sure he'd had one since sinking a taproot, or trying to, in Apache Springs.

He woke twice to the jiggling of his doorknob. He didn't know who it was out there in the hall, and he didn't want to know.

Of course, he knew. It was either one or both of the Kosgrove sisters. He knew Emma was staying in town tonight, too. She no longer had a canyon and an ancient church to watch over.

It was going to take a long time for Yakima to forget both sisters. He loved them both in different ways. But he might as well start the forgetting tonight. Apache Springs had outgrown him, become fraught with way too many complications.

He rose before dawn, skipped breakfast and coffee, and saddled Wolf in the pre-dawn dark, hearing Gramps Dawson snoring in his sleeping quarters in the lean-to off the livery barn proper.

He rode past the town marshal's office on the way out of town. He stopped when he saw Galveston Penny sitting on the raised gallery fronting the place, running an oiled rag down his Winchester.

The young deputy stopped his work to gaze into the pearling shadows at the big, dark, long-haired man sitting the big black stallion before him. Yakima had thrown out the nice suit he'd been wearing while wearing the badge. He'd exchanged it for his old trail clothes—skintight, wash-worn denim trousers, calico shirt, and the bear claw necklace he'd fashioned from a grizzly he'd killed and which had nearly killed him a few years back. He wore it as a talisman of sorts, though he didn't know if he believed in such things.

After the treasure-laden canyon, he didn't know what he believed anymore...

His stag-butted Colt .44 was holstered on his thigh,

his Bowie knife sheathed on his waist, and his short but deadly Arkansas toothpick positioned in the thin leather holster behind his neck.

His Winchester Yellowboy repeater, a gift from the Chaolin monk he'd once laid track with even longer ago than his meeting with the bear...even before the beloved and unforgettable Faith had come into his life, enriching it immeasurably before she'd died...was snugged down in his rifle boot.

Galveston cleared his throat and climbed to his feet. "You...leavin' now, Mar...I mean, Yakima?"

Yakima nodded. "Been good knowin' you, Galveston. Take care of yourself. Take care of the Rio Grande Kid, too."

Galveston smiled. "I sure will." He paused, frowned. "Where you goin'...if I ain't bein' too snoopy, that is...?"

"I'd love to tell you...if I knew myself."

Yakima smiled, pinched his hat brim to the young man, and rode along the fresh rails. At the edge of town, he met a train howling into Apache Springs, and he poked his fingers into his ears to mute the infernal, caterwauling din.

God damn "progress", anyway...

He headed west, away from the rising sun, as though the sun was his past and there was any way in hell a man could outrun it.

A Look At: Redemption Trail: A Yakima Henry Western

Lifelong loner Yakima Henry unexpectedly befriends Paul Cahill, an old prospector with roots in a once-wealthy Eastern family. When Cahill is mortally wounded by men stalking his and Yakima's trail, Cahill asks Yakima to travel to northern Dakota Territory and deliver a letter and a belt stuffed with money to his estranged son.

On his trip north, Yakima befriends two young sisters whose mother has died and who, escaping an abusive stepfather, are trying to make their way north to their grandparents' farm along the Cannon Ball River. Heading into owlhoot-infested Dakota Territory is no nap in the shade for Yaikma alone but traveling with two complicated young women is no picnic, either.

When an Irish countess seduces Yakima, enflaming her husband's jealous rage, and the bounty-hunting assassin called The Reverend stalks Yakima's and the girls' trail, Yakima comes to believe that when his friend Paul sent him north to Dakota, he'd really been sending him hell-bound!

AVAILABLE NOW

ABOUT THE AUTHOR

Peter Brandvold grew up in the great state of North Dakota in the 1960's and '70s, when television westerns were as popular as shows about hoarders and shark tanks are now, and western paperbacks were as popular as Game of Thrones.

Brandvold watched every western series on television at the time. He grew up riding horses and herding cows on the farms of his grandfather and many friends who owned livestock.

Brandvold's imagination has always lived and will always live in the West. He is the author of over a hundred lightning-fast action westerns under his own name and his pen name, Frank Leslie.

CPSIA information can be obtained
at www.ICGtesting.com
Printed in the USA
LVHW100821241121
704098LV00011B/534

9 781647 346263